Jericho
A Historical
Novel

Gwen Chermack

ISBN: 069225871X
ISBN-13: 978-0692258712
Published by Outstanding Publications
(www.OutstandingPublicationscom)

Also by Gwen Chermack

Restoration: A Tale of Redemption, Available from Amazon as well as Barnes and Noble.

Restoration tells the story of Liz Durant, homeless and hopeless in a strange city, finds herself face to face with a cop and his friend who want to give her a chance to get on her feet again.

- Can she get beyond her past and allow them to be tools of restoration in her life?

- Can God actually care about her?

- Can He be reaching out to her through these wonderful people?

- Is she really open to His restoration in her life?

Believing that God has forsaken her, Liz runs away from her hurt and ends up living on the streets. In a case of mistaken identity, Liz finds herself being helped by two Christian men. Working her way back into society and finding herself working in the last place she thought - a church - Liz begins to find God's love. This story is a love story - not of just a man and a woman, but of finding oneself in love with the Creator and recognizing His unwavering love.

TABLE OF CONTENTS

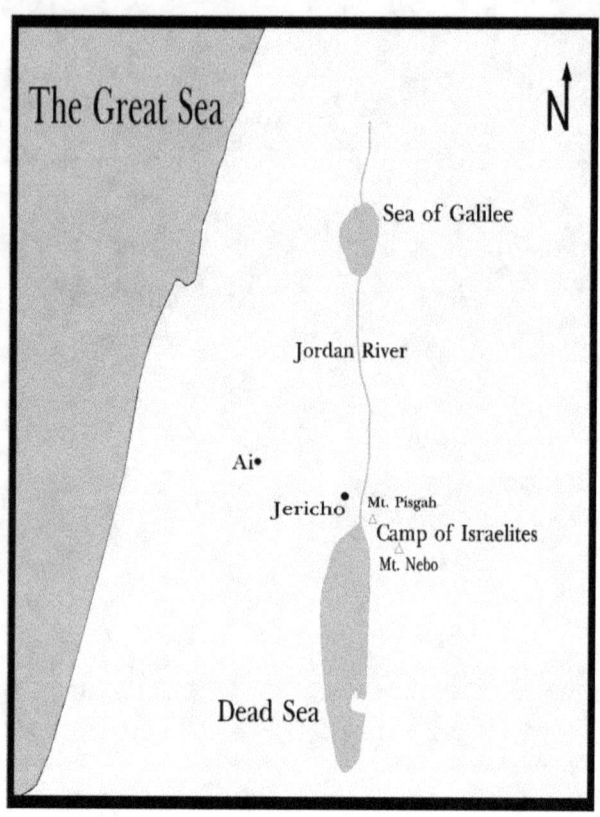

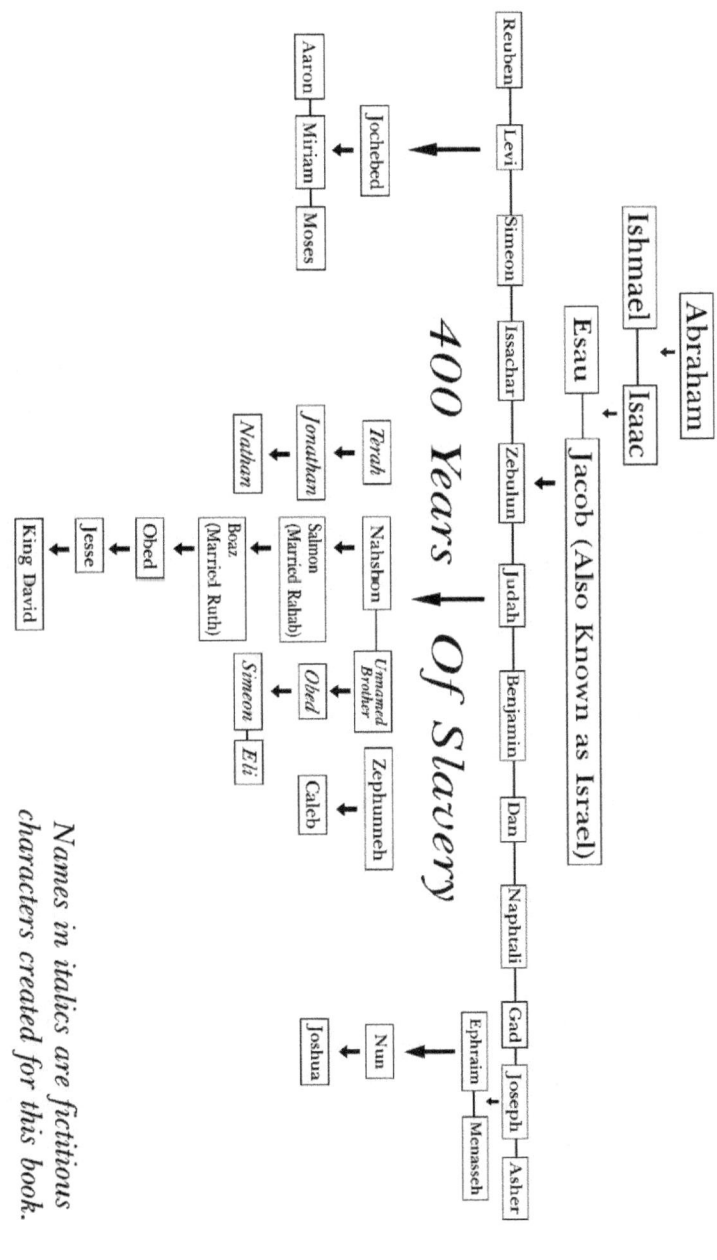

Names in italics are fictitious characters created for this book.

1
THE FIFTH SON OF OBED

Dust swirled around sandaled feet. The two men continued to wrestle, ignoring the choking in their throats and grit scratching at their eyes. Both were determined to win this impromptu match, each for unique reasons. Even as an adult, Simeon longed to see the approval on his father's face. Nathan hoped to impress Rebekkah's father.

Simeon was taller by a handbreadth, but Nathan was stocky and strong. The two had wrestled many times before, and the score was nearly even. The men who had gathered around to watch cheered both of them loudly, regardless of which one had the upper hand.

"Good move Nathan," one man would shout, and then follow that immediately with, "Way to stop him, Simeon!"

Obed however, stood stiff and critical. He was not cheering for either of the men, in spite of being Simeon's father. This was not surprising, as he was a harsh man who demanded much of his offspring.

Shortly before Simeon was born, an angel visited Obed in a dream, announcing that this child, his fifth son, would be a man of great faith. The day of Simeon's birth, Obed confidently proclaimed, "This tiny infant will be instrumental in Adonai's plan for our tribe and our people." His family and friends had rejoiced with him.

So far, Simeon had not lived up to his father's expectations. Aside from his appearance - tall, slender, and handsome - he seemed altogether average among the throngs of young men camped in the wilderness waiting for Moses and Joshua to lead them into the land God had promised to Abraham and his descendants.

Perhaps thinking people were critical of Simeon's lack of accomplishment, Obed was quick to remind anyone who would listen that they were of the tribe of Judah. His uncle, Nahshon had the great honor of representing the people of Judah, and was the first one to present an offering in the new tabernacle.

On this sunny, arid day, Simeon knew Obed was hoping his son would make him proud by wrestling Nathan down quickly and easily. That was not happening. On the contrary, Nathan was holding his ground with the tenacity of an unmoving donkey.

Simeon had just gotten a good hold on Nathan's wrist, and was about to spin him around, when the distant sound of trumpets was heard above the noise of the crowd of onlookers.

Nathan and Simeon instantly relaxed their hold on each other. The men being entertained by the spontaneous wrestling match stiffened and looked about with surprise on their faces. Simeon wondered if somehow they had forgotten that it was the Sabbath, but discarded that notion quickly. These were not ram's horn shofars they heard, but the two silver trumpets.

"Who sounded the signal calling the congregation to the Tent of Meeting, and why would they do such a thing on this hot morning?" Simeon wondered aloud.

Nathan and Simeon stepped in line with the others and picked their way through hundreds of tents to the Tabernacle, near where Moses was camped. Throughout the past forty years in this wasteland, they gathered at the Tent of Meeting whenever the trumpets were blown to signal an assembly of the tribes. As they approached, excitement crackled in the air.

Life in the wilderness didn't hold a tremendous amount of adventure for the Hebrews. Aside from the occasional wild animal that strayed too close to camp looking for a tasty morsel, the only thing that provided relief from the boredom was the daily combat training for every man of fighting age.

Simeon loved learning to fight, and enjoyed sparring with Nathan more than anyone else. Growing up with four older brothers, he had learned to defend himself early in life. He was much better at hand-to-hand combat than with a sword, a fact Nathan reminded him of regularly.

Hopeful that he would soon get to put his skills into practice, and wondering what thrilling news Moses had to announce, Simeon walked with a spring in his step and anticipation in his heart.

+-+-+-+

Zidon leaned against the red silken pillow in the corner, his brooding eyes taking all of her in with one fluid glance. "When are you going to marry me?" he asked with a playful grin.

"When the goddess Astarte comes to life and tells me to," she replied with an equally playful sparkle in her eye. She began to get dressed, her back to him.

"Oh, come on, Rahab. Why are you so loyal to her? Astarte is just a bronze idol on a street corner. I am flesh and blood, and I love you!" he admitted, leaning toward her.

Quickly standing to her feet, Rahab walked toward the door. "Astarte is MY god. Until she, or a god greater than her, tells me to stop my way of living, I'll go right on doing what I have always done." Her voice softened a bit, "If there was anyone I might consider changing my profession for, it would be you, Zidon, but I just don't love you like that. I'm sorry."

Shaking his head, he tried to look hurt as he pretended to stab himself with an imaginary knife. "OW! OW!" She couldn't help but chuckle at his silliness.

"I had hoped that you might have changed your mind since the last time I asked," he laughed, "but somehow I knew better than to get my hopes up."

He stood and began putting his clothes on. "You can't blame a guy for trying. You are the most beautiful woman in Jericho. I'd actually think about giving up my commission for you."

Rahab looked at him with a soft smile on her face. "Zidon, we both know that you love being a soldier more than you could ever love a woman. I'm too smart to get hooked up with you."

"Hey, that almost hurt," he called back over his shoulder from the doorway, "I'll see you next time I can get away for a while."

Crossing the threshold into the bright daylight, he put on his helmet. *At least this time she didn't make fun of me for my helmet*, he thought. *It's taller than the other soldiers' because the King considers me more important than them. There's nothing funny about that.*

Grateful for that hour he got to spend with Rahab, Zidon turned the corner and headed back toward the palace. He slowed as he passed the idol of Astarte. It wasn't much taller than a cubit. She was standing nude with only a pearl necklace, a lily, and a serpent for adornments. *How unfeminine for her to be holding a serpent*, he thought. *The lily I understand, all women enjoy flowers. But a serpent?*

He then noticed her horned hat for the first time. It was very tall and lofty appearing. He liked the way it looked, and it made him somehow feel closer to her. His helmet was not nearly as disproportionately tall as her hat, and Rahab never made fun of her.

Maybe she just teases me out of affection, he thought as he smiled. *Well, if she believes so strongly in Astarte, it can't hurt for me to say a prayer to her also.*

He bowed slightly and quietly said, "Oh great goddess Astarte, please soften Rahab's heart toward me. Please appear to Rahab. Tell her to marry me, and I will call you *my* god, too."

His brief prayer gave him hope, and he whistled an upbeat tune as he rounded the corner and headed toward the palace. *I'll ask her again next week*, he decided happily.

+-+-+-+

While walking toward the tent of meeting, off to one side, Simeon could hear a young mother talking softly to her small daughter, "We are going to see Moses. Do you remember who he is?"

He slowed down to listen, curious about how the little girl would respond.

"Moses is the one who brought the Law down from Sinai," she said with wonder on her tiny face. Her mother responded, "Yes, and he's preparing us to enter Canaan, the land Adonai promised to Abraham."

The teeming crowd then swallowed them up, just as the mother was explaining how the land is full of wicked people such as the Amorites, Hittites, and Perrizites.

Simeon was disappointed not to hear the best part of the story. He always got a charge when he heard how the Children of Israel were going to dispossess the evil people of their land. He couldn't wait for that part of their destiny, and he hoped it would come to pass before the new moon.

Eventually, the people settled in around the Tent of Meeting. They stood anxiously waiting for their leader to emerge from his tent. Over the years, as the crowd glimpsed Moses' face, they hushed in awe. Today was no exception as expectant silence washed across the assembly.

Perhaps this would be the day God would have them move into Canaan, defeat the pagans, and inherit the land. Anticipation was palpable as Nathan's eyes briefly met Simeon's in an excited glance.

Simeon stood on his toes, scanning the sea of people, searching for his father, but was unable to see him from where he stood. They had gotten separated along the way, and he breathed a sigh of relief to be out from under Obed's critical glare, even if only for a short while.

A scowl covered his face as he thought, *it seems as though nothing I ever do is good enough to make my father proud of me.* Sensing expectation from those around him, he suppressed those thoughts for the time being.

The anticipation of finally moving into the Promised Land was overwhelming. He attempted to keep his mind on what was at hand, but the prospect of tasting foods he had only been told about, and seeing vines that actually grow fruit, which were now merely figments of his imagination, made it difficult for him to concentrate. His mind was overflowing with visions of what Canaan would look like, and how it would taste, smell, and feel.

Every morning he would think, *today could be* the *day*. He would prepare himself to hear the silver trumpets summoning the tribes to the Tent of Meeting for the big declaration. Every night, he'd go to bed thinking, *tomorrow could be* the *day*.

This morning, the trumpets were actually blown. The tribes were all assembled. It was so exciting!

Simeon was grateful to be taller than most men, especially today. He had a nearly unobstructed view of Moses and Joshua as they emerged from the tent. They both appeared extremely serious. Moses looked as though he had a death to announce.

This was not what Simeon had hoped to see. Apparently this meeting wouldn't be the announcement of a timeline and battle plan for their entrance into Canaan. He fought back disappointment.

Moses' voice cut through the silence of over one million eager listeners. It was still surprisingly strong for his age, and even from their distant position, Nathan and Simeon could make out nearly every word.

Simeon shook his head, wondering if he really heard Moses say that he was 120 years old today. He knew better than to ask Nathan. Out of sheer respect, when Moses spoke, not another sound was heard.

Moses loudly proclaimed, "Joshua, son of Nun, is to be your new leader." This was a highly anticipated appointment, and Simeon was pleased to have it finally be official. Around the campfires at night, there would be no more second guessing who Moses would choose.

Turning and placing his hands on Joshua, Moses prophesied, "Be strong and of good courage, for you will bring the children of Israel into the land which I swore to them, and I will be with you."

Since Joshua and Caleb had spied out the land forty years ago, they had been respected and revered. God had spared their lives because they had trusted in His promise. Now He was promoting Joshua to the highest place of leadership.

Joshua had been Moses' assistant from his youth. Moses had even changed his name from Hoshea to Joshua, meaning "Adonai Is Salvation." Lately, it seemed as though no one ever saw one without the other. The two had become inseparable. The announcement of Joshua's succession did not come as a surprise to anyone. After reviewing the Law and teaching the congregation a song, Moses and Joshua headed up toward Mount Nebo.

Simeon and Nathan stood still for a few extra moments, quietly watching the two men of God walk away. Nathan broke the silence, "It's amazing Moses is still so spry. Can you believe he's 120 years old?" Simeon grinned and nodded his head in agreement; grateful he didn't have to ask for confirmation.

The people gradually dispersed, returning to their previous activities. Excitement about seeing Moses was still evident, and there was a hum of stimulated chatter.

Simeon slapped Nathan on the back playfully, "So, are you up for finishing our wrestling match, or would you rather concede and be done with it?" Nathan, with a twinkle in his eye, replied, "I'd sooner be the first one into the first city needing to be defeated in the Promised Land. I wouldn't dream of quitting. I was obviously winning!"

Laughing heartily, Simeon threw his arm around the shoulder of his dearest friend, and they walked back toward their tents to settle the matter.

2
DEATH OF THE MAN OF GOD

Nathan had soundly beaten Simeon in the second half of their wrestling match. Obed was not present to see it, and for this, Simeon was grateful. Rebekkah's father had been nearby, but everyone else was concerned with the appointment of Joshua as leader. A simple wrestling match that had been a point of interest earlier that day now seemed relatively insignificant.

Moses was preparing them for his death, and for the day Joshua would completely assume leadership of over one million descendants of Abraham. It was obvious Moses was getting old, but he seemed to be in such good health that they all agreed it might not be any time soon.

Moses and Joshua had a tendency to disappear for significant periods of time when they left the camp together, so the Israelites had developed a laid back attitude. It was thought there would be some time before they had to pick up and move again.

Simeon watched as dusk approached, campfires were prepared, and little ones begged their parents to stay up a bit later. Assuming this would be an ordinary, uneventful evening, the parents were succumbing to their persistent requests. The fire rings were dotted with dozing children snuggled up on parents" laps.

The calm of the evening was shattered by the piercing sound of trumpets cutting through the relaxed chatter. Simeon had a gut feeling that this wasn't a good sign. *Moses and Joshua are back already?* A jumble of questions racing through his mind, Simeon hastily dropped dried dung and firewood he had been gathering into the ring and sprinted toward the Tent of Meeting.

Approaching the Tent, he could hear a faint sound as if people were wailing. The closer he got, the louder it became. By the time he arrived, breathless, at a spot where he could actually see Joshua, the sound was deafening. A tear-streaked Joshua was standing on the hill, holding Moses' tunic and the staff he had lifted when God parted the Red Sea.

The reality of it hit Simeon. He cried out, his voice melting in with one million others in a chorus of noise that was coming from deep within the people. This could only mean one thing. The adopted grandson of the Pharaoh, the great deliverer of the Hebrew people, the man who spoke with God face to face, was now dead.

+-+-+-+

Zidon lay perfectly still, afraid to move, for fear of waking Rahab. He studied her features as she slept. *She looks so peaceful. Almost like a sleeping child,* he thought.

He admired her high cheekbones and perfectly shaped eyebrows. Just as his eyes lit upon her lips, she jumped as if startled. Her eyes shot open and she drew a quick breath.

"Oh, it's just you." She relaxed and took a few long breaths.

"Just me?" He was hurt by her comment, but didn't want to show it.

"I'm sorry. I didn't mean it that way. I guess I was dreaming. I'm glad it's 'just' you." She kissed his forehead and stood to her feet.

After several awkward moments, as he debated if he should pursue the matter, he queried, "Who were you expecting?"

"I wasn't expecting anyone. It was just a bad dream." She stood, and glanced out the window. "When do you have to be back to the palace?"

"I'm off for the rest of the day, why?"

"Let's go for a walk. I'll pack a lunch and we can go to the Jordan River." Excitement sparkled in her eyes.

Rahab was always ready to go on an adventure. Any time the sun was out and she wasn't expecting any customers, one could find her climbing a hillside or swimming in the river. She loved the outdoors. Her enthusiasm was contagious.

"There's only one condition, though," she added, "you have to leave your silly helmet here. I won't be seen with you wearing it outside the city." She smiled as she began to gather food for their outing.

It was the moment he had been waiting for all week. "I'll have you know," he replied, "*Your* goddess Astarte is wearing a hat that is much taller than mine."

"Nonsense," she replied, shaking her head strongly. "Her hat can't be any taller than my little finger." She giggled before she finished saying it.

He failed to see why she continued to find it funny, and replied rather dryly, "Proportionately!" Again, she laughed at his lack of humor.

"Why are you so sensitive about a silly helmet?" She asked as she neared the door with her basket of fruit.

"I wish you would take my position seriously. You could quit taking in customers." They stepped into the bright daylight. "You could stop having bad dreams about those customers. You could rest easy, knowing you are loved and taken care of." They strolled down the street as he continued.

"The King has put me in a position where I could easily provide for you. All it would take is one word from you, and it would be done."

About that time, they rounded the corner and came upon the idol of Astarte. Rahab stopped, mumbled a few words, bowed slightly, and kissed the idol. She then stood back up, looked at Zidon, and said, "You are right."

Zidon could not believe his ears. His heart nearly skipped a beat as his brain quickly processed what she just said. He had never gotten her to even consider marrying him. He wondered what had been the magic words he had used today. He almost couldn't contain his excitement.

"Her hat *is* taller than my little finger." Rahab finished the sentence, nodded her head, and walked down the street with a giggle.

+-+-+-+

Never had Simeon seen or heard such mourning. Well into the darkness of night, the sobbing over Moses' death continued. The dust the mourners threw on their heads as a sign of their grief swirled around in the air.

Simeon left earlier than most. He needed time to process the events of the day, and dejectedly wandered off to the hills to be by himself.

He was struck by the intensity of the mourning. Certainly, Moses had been a great leader to his people, but most of them had never met him, never even spoken to him. Simeon was one of the many who had only seen Moses from a distance. He was distressed over Moses' death, but was not grieving as deeply as many of the others.

Nearly all the Hebrews had murmured and complained about Moses, but now he was gone, and they had no way of apologizing for their lack of respect. Possibly, the mourners were seeing the error in their attitudes. *Hopefully*, Simeon thought, *there is some repentance in the midst of the lamentations.*

Simeon knew most people had been waiting to see whether or not Moses could indeed prepare them to conquer the Promised Land. Some theorized he had gotten too old; others said he was inordinately caught up in the tabernacle and priesthood. Many others agreed he had become overly involved in the civil affairs of the congregation.

Regardless of their view of Moses' leadership, there was apprehensive talk of how the Promised Land really was populated with giants, and that their relatively easy victories over the Kings Sihon and Og were not an adequate measurement of how it might go once they had crossed the Jordan, and were actually in the land of Canaan.

As Simeon considered the life of Moses; the great feats he had performed, the glow on his face as he would come out of the presence of God, and the way he led the people with dignity despite the constant criticism, Simeon thought of his own father.

Obed had not criticized Moses any time that Simeon could remember. If he ever heard anyone who did, Obed would issue a loud rebuke. The people quickly learned not to invite him around if there was any chance Moses would come up in the conversation. Obed loved and respected his leader, and actually met him once. He prayed for Moses every day. He would not tolerate anything but that same deep-seated respect for authority from his own children.

Simeon knew it was partially due to their tribal affiliation. Many embraced the view that Jacob's dying words indicated the Messiah would come from the tribe of Judah. "The scepter will not depart from Judah, nor a lawgiver from between his feet until Shiloh comes, and to Him will be the obedience of all the people."

Obed was certain that Jacob intended it as a prophecy of their Deliverer. He recognized that his own people would maintain a place in history, and he did his best to live up to that expectation. He also instructed his household to strive toward that same goal.

Simeon realized tears were streaming down his face again, but this time not in mourning for Moses, but rather out of thankfulness for Obed. His father had trained him in such a way that he had no regrets about his own attitude toward Moses.

Leaning against a large boulder in the moonlight, with his mind jumping back and forth from Moses to his father to Joshua and the Promised Land, Simeon drifted off to sleep.

3
PERIOD OF MOURNING

The cycle of the moon following Moses' death was the Hebrew's period of mourning. Nothing but respect for the deceased was permitted. Around their campfires, the evenings were full of people reminiscing about the tremendous things he had accomplished.

It was during one of those evenings at the campfire that Simeon thought back to the last time he saw Moses, his brother Aaron, and sister Miriam together. It had been the day they were told to move into the Wilderness of Zin and camp at Kadesh.

At the time, the thought had crossed Simeon's mind that maybe God would relent and let them all three enter the Promised Land together. It seemed unfair of a "just God" to punish them along with the other people. Not only were they related to Moses, but also Aaron was the high priest and Miriam had cared for Moses non-stop. Simeon wondered if they too had complained about their brother, deciding that they must have done so at some point.

He often pondered the accounts his mother shared with him as a child, of how all the people grumbled and complained about Moses, about their food, and about how they felt mistreated by God. Admittedly, they would have preferred to remain as slaves in Egypt, where at least food and water were readily available. They distrusted God and His promise of their own land flowing with milk and honey.

When Moses sent twelve spies to scout out Canaan, the grumbling people chose to accept the report of ten of them. These ten men described the inhabitants as giants who could not be defeated. The Children of Israel even tried to stone the other two, Joshua and Caleb, for their unwavering faith that Adonai had truly given them the land.

Even though he was born years after the fact, Simeon harbored a childhood wish that somehow he could have been one of the spies sent into the land. As a young man, he and Nathan frequently found long, straight sticks, which became make-believe swords to kill the Amorites.

He had such faith in God's promise, he was certain his report would have aligned with Joshua and Caleb. *If I could have been one of the spies, three of us would have been in agreement that we could indeed possess the land, giants or not. Maybe then the people might have accepted the challenge,* Simeon lamented. Instead, the Children of Israel had accused Moses of bringing them into the wilderness just to die.

God wearied of hearing their murmuring and announced through Moses, "Just as you have spoken in My hearing, so I will do to you. According to the number of days in which you spied out the land, forty days, for each day you will bear your guilt one year, namely forty years, and you will know My rejection."

"The carcasses of you who have complained against Me will fall in the wilderness, all of you who were numbered from twenty years old and above. But your little ones, whom you said would be victims, I will bring in, and they will know the land which you have despised."

Simeon could recall as many as fifty people dying in one day. Mounds of burial stones were everywhere. Miriam died shortly after they arrived at Kadesh, and Aaron died on Mount Hor. Neither was to see the Promised Land.

Simeon was left to assume they had grumbled, and deserved judgment along with the others. He was grateful his parents were both young enough to be spared. Once again, he vowed, *I will never complain or murmur about how things appear to be going.*

Only the people who had been at least five or six years old at the time of the forty year verdict remembered the days of slavery in Egypt, the plagues, the deliverance, the parting of the Red Sea, water coming from the rock, the Commandments being given at Sinai, and the other great miracles performed before the judgment and the wandering.

Those people nearest to sixty were surrounded like dignitaries. Having been nearly twenty at the exodus, their memories were far more vivid, with greater detail, and given from the perspective of an adult. Everyone repeatedly wanted to hear eyewitness accounts of those miraculous events. Even though the vast majority were born in the wilderness, they joined into the conversations as though they themselves had experienced the miracles. It was "us" and "we," "our people," "my tribe," "our clan."

Simeon immensely enjoyed the stories and was saddened that the thirty days of mourning would soon be coming to a close. Thinking back, he could not ever remember going this long without hearing a solitary word of murmuring or complaining. Without all the negativity, people seemed more satisfied with their surroundings, with the manna, with the leadership, and everything in general.

He found it interesting that through the death of His servant Moses, God moved people to repent of bad attitudes, to be grateful for their provisions, and to get along with one another, even if only for a brief period. His mother often commented, "We find Adonai easiest through a tragedy, for it is then that we are willing to seek Him."

Simeon hoped this outlook would continue as they moved toward Canaan to conquer the giants, and possess the promise given to Abraham over 500 years prior. Unfortunately, as the last day of mourning drew to a close and people were preparing the evening fires, he could already sense discontentment resurfacing.

+-+-+-+

Zidon and Rahab left the city and walked toward the Jordan River. She was swinging the basket of fruit, and almost skipping. He liked to see her out in the country like this. She was much happier here than inside the city. He knew that in her heart, she would much rather live in a tent like the nomads, than in the noisy, crowded streets of Jericho.

Sitting on rocks at the edge of the river, splashing their feet in the water, they ate grapes and figs.

"Have you ever noticed the difference between the Jordan upstream and down?" She asked as she squinted her eyes against the reflection off the water.

Zidon wasn't sure how to respond. "Um, the water upstream is not here yet, and the water downstream has already passed us?" He hoped she would laugh at his attempted joke, but was disappointed to find that it was a rhetorical question.

"The water upstream is part of the Sea of Galilee. It flows right past us into the Dead Sea. Don't you find that odd?" She looked at him for an answer this time.

"I'm not following you," he admitted.

"Well, the Sea of Galilee is full of life. The fishermen have no problems filling their nets. It is a thriving lake." She popped a couple grapes into her mouth.

"The Dead Sea, on the other hand, is dead. Nothing lives in it." She paused, looking at him expectantly.

"So far this is not a big revelation, Rahab." He was shaking his head back and forth with a confused look on his face.

"Don't you see? The river flows into the Sea of Galilee at the top, and out of the Sea of Galilee toward us. There is life there!" She got so excited that she jumped up off of her rock before continuing. "The river then flows directly into the Dead Sea which has no outlet. There is *no* life there!"

He thought for several moments, desperately attempting to decipher the deeper meaning behind the path of the Jordan River. Unable to do so, he sat in silence waiting for the explanation.

"We are sitting between life and death; right here in Jericho." She paused as if thinking hard about what she was going to say next. "If we take what we are given and give it to someone else, we continue to breed more life like the Sea of Galilee. If we take in life and don't pass it along, we'll die like the Dead Sea. We are at the crossroads!"

Zidon sat in silence, lost in thought, until he felt cold water in his face. She had waded into the river, scooped up a handful, and thrown it at him. She was already laughing and running toward the city so he could not retaliate.

He grabbed the empty food basket and sprinted after her, with a look of affection on his face.

4
THE OUTBURST

The Israelite people were giving their best count, speculating exactly which day would complete the fortieth year. The numbers differed by a factor of several months. This wasn't surprising, considering the majority of the people discussing the matter were not even born the day it was announced. Regardless, everyone seemed to agree on one thing; it should be either just recently passed, or very soon to come.

Now that the 30 days of mourning had come to an end, he heard the other men say things like, "Joshua doesn't know what to do. He's a military man, not a leader," and "Sure, Joshua distinguished himself at the battle with the Amalakites, but that was a long time ago."

Every one of them had watched Moses lay hands on him and tell him to be bold and strong, the Lord would be with him. They all heard the words spoken over him, watched him go into the Tent of Meeting with Moses, and saw Adonai himself descend in the cloud of smoke. *Why have the outspoken ones forgotten those things so readily?* Simeon wondered.

A slow angry flush came over Simeon as he heard the grumblings and growing dissatisfaction among these men who only a few weeks ago had praised Moses' chosen appointment.

He could no longer hold his tongue. He jumped up from his rock near the campfire, "I'm tired of hearing you all complain about Joshua! He's the one Adonai has chosen to lead us. Who are we to tell God that His choice is inadequate?"

Simeon's voice grew even stronger as he stood tall, hands clenched. "Don't you remember when Moses said that as God was with him, so God would be with Joshua? Have you forgotten how he and Caleb stood against the other ten spies in the face of stoning, and still kept their faith and trust in Adonai?"

By now every person within earshot was focused on Simeon. "You watched him win battles through the strength and wisdom given to him by Adonai. How can you still not trust the God who feeds you every morning with bread from heaven? You people of little faith!"

The crowd was hushed as the words "little faith" rang in their ears. Standing in utter silence, Simeon realized he had spoken much louder than intended. People several campfires over were looking in his direction to see who was offering such a thunderous, impassioned rebuke.

A red-faced Simeon felt a hand on his arm. He turned to see Nathan beside him. Although he didn't utter a word, the reality of him standing in a show of approval and solidarity was enough to keep Simeon from crumpling in embarrassment. His eyes dropped to the men sitting at the fire he was standing near, yet not a person returned his gaze. They were all looking into the fire. Simeon hoped this was out of shame for their harsh words against Joshua.

Each man slowly stood, making his way back to his own tent, careful to avoid eye contact with Simeon or Nathan. The two friends remained standing until nearly every fire ring they could see was abandoned. Only a few others had stood with them, indicating agreement, but most had gone to bed with their heads hanging.

Simeon and Nathan eventually sat back down on their rocks in the prevailing silence. Not a word had been spoken since Simeon's booming proclamation "You people of little faith!" He found comfort in the wood crackling and flames dancing in front of him.

Finally Nathan broke the silence, "You sounded so much like your father. I bet he would have been pleased to hear you stand up for Joshua." Simeon continued staring silently into the flames, thinking how grateful he was that Obed hadn't been present. Surely by now, his father had already heard half a dozen accounts of the reproof.

Every man at the fire except Nathan was older than Simeon. He had openly rebuked men whom he was admonished to respect and obey. *I am certain he would have been disappointed in me*, Simeon thought. *Not with what I said, but whom I said it to.* Simeon felt his father always managed to find fault with what his son did, and this time, he figured the censure would be well deserved.

Not knowing what to say, they continued in silence until an elderly stranger asked if he might rest a while at their fire. Nathan and Simeon both welcomed him, and he slowly lowered his obviously tired body carefully onto one of the rocks. In the shifting glow of the firelight, Simeon found it difficult to make out the man's features. *He definitely has a warm smile. I like him already.* Simeon decided.

He appeared to be one of the men who barely escaped God's judgment. *Actually, he appears too old to still be alive,* Simeon thought, studying the man a little closer. He definitely looked older than 60, but maybe it was the lack of light that made him seem so ancient.

Where do I know him from? Simeon thought. He seemed familiar, but not enough to put his finger on when or where he had encountered this man before.

"Did either of you young men witness the lecture earlier this evening?" He questioned. Simeon quickly stole a glance at Nathan. "I hear he scolded them thoroughly, reprimanding them as men of 'little faith.'"

Expecting discipline from the stranger, Simeon began to hang his head when something welled up inside him, and he was filled with indignation again. He lifted his head, stuck his chin out, threw back his shoulders, and proudly said, "We were indeed witnesses. I am the one who called them 'men of little faith,' and that's precisely what they are." Having restated his position, he softened a bit, "Do you disagree with what I said?"

The stranger chuckled as he assured them he had no issue with it. Simeon relaxed a little and waited for the man to explain his inquiry. The dignified gentleman sat for a moment, with that warm smile tugging at the corners of his mouth as he concentrated beyond the flames dancing at his feet. Simeon got the impression he was praying.

After what seemed like a very long time, he asked both of them to accompany him back to his tent. Out of respect for someone elderly, and curious about his strange request, they were obliged to agree.

As they walked, he asked them how they felt about going into the land of the Amorites and Canaanites soon. At this question, Nathan finally spoke up, "I'm ready to face any giant they have, providing Adonai is with me!"

"You may get the chance to do that much sooner than you think, young man, much sooner than you think," the old man's voice trailed off until it was nearly inaudible. The two glanced at each other, puzzled by what this man was saying.

The further they walked, the closer they got to where Moses' tent had been. Neither of them had ever seen which tent belonged to whom, but Simeon's heart rate was steadily increasing as they drew near the edge of the camp at the base of Mount Nebo. He and Nathan exchanged nervous glances again, and Simeon began to suspect they were headed for Joshua to be reprimanded for disrespecting his elders, despite the assurance the man had given him back at the campfire.

His palms began to sweat, even though it was a chilly evening. A brief glance at Nathan revealed huge eyes and a very pale face. Wondering if his friend was going to faint, Simeon felt badly for getting him into this.

Nathan was not the type to pick a fight, but once engaged, he was never one to walk away from it. He was more perseverant than anyone Simeon had ever encountered. Gratitude for his best friend welled up inside him and he silently thanked God for blessing him with Nathan.

None of them had spoken for quite some time now. Simeon wondered if the stranger was secretly enjoying their discomfort. Eventually they stopped outside a tent. The elderly man turned to them with a kind countenance. Confirming Simeon's worst fears, he said, "Please wait here. Joshua will see you shortly." With that he turned and disappeared into the entrance, leaving Simeon and Nathan bewildered and alone.

+-+-+-+

Putting his arm around Rahab, Zidon requested that she stay on the bed with him a bit longer. She relaxed and asked, "What is bothering you, Zidon?"

"I'm going to tell you something because I trust you. You cannot tell anyone about what I share with you." His eyes searched hers for acknowledgement of a pact. Rahab nodded her head in agreement.

"It is likely that we will soon be invaded by the Hebrews." He paused, waiting for the gravity of the situation to sink in.

"Who are the Hebrews?" she asked naively.

"Who are the Hebrews?" he repeated in disbelief. "They are the desert people from across the Jordan!" He waited for a reaction, but got none. "There are over one million Hebrews," he continued, "and they have defeated Sihon and Og. We are afraid Jericho is next."

He could now see the concern on Rahab's face. "But our wall," she said with her voice shaking, "isn't it secure?" Zidon slowly shook his head, not wanting to admit the facts.

"We have been told since childhood that nobody can penetrate our city wall. We have been assured of our absolute safety. Now you tell me that isn't true?" She accused, alarm in her voice.

Zidon thought for a moment about how to phrase his next statement. Nothing soothing came to mind, so he just blurted out. "There are over one million of them! They could defeat us just with sheer numbers." He felt a chill run down his spine. "They annihilated the Amorites under Sihon and Og. Our wall is legendary, but I'm afraid it is not enough."

Rahab had turned away from him and was looking out the window as he continued. "The King is doubling our training duty. He's posted guards at strategic spots in the city to watch for any sign of them. He's commissioned Rekem to send out reconnaissance teams to gather as much information as possible."

Rahab's eyes dropped to the floor in front of her. "Rekem is a wise choice. He's a slimy little guy," she stated very matter-of-factly, "and will do a good job of sneaking around."

Zidon almost laughed, but then realized that the only way she could know Rekem would be in a "professional" capacity. He didn't want to think about the woman he loved with that obsequious snake, so he kept talking about the Hebrews to keep his mind off of it.

"All the soldiers have been given strict orders to watch for anyone who looks like he might have come in from the desert. We are to report directly to the King if we locate someone suspicious."

He lowered his voice, not wanting to admit what he was about to say. "I'm convinced they are going to attempt a surprise attack."

"Our gods will protect us." Rahab stated.

"They don't serve gods like we do. They only serve one God. All one million people! Only one God! Imagine that! Amazing!" He shook his head and sighed.

"This God of theirs is powerful and mighty," Consternation blanketed his face as he continued. "I've heard that He killed all of Pharaoh's soldiers and not one Hebrew had to lift a finger. There are rumors that He sends them bread to eat every morning." He shook his head in disbelief. "They say that He can make water appear from solid stone, and also dried up the water of the Red Sea. This is no ordinary God the Hebrew people serve."

Looking up, he found Rahab fearfully searching his face with tears in her eyes. He put his arms around her, allowing her to cry on his shoulder.

"I'm sorry I scared you," he said tenderly, "but I thought you should have the chance to prepare yourself." He stroked the long jet-black hair cascading down her back.

"I must admit, I'm concerned about you living here in this house against the wall. You have a window that their soldiers could easily get into with a ladder. You cannot stay here."

He held her tighter. "Please marry me," he was now pleading with her. "I'll protect you from the Hebrews with my very life. Don't be stubborn. Marry me."

He continued to hold her while she finished crying. She raised her head and he almost gasped. She had cried most of her face paint off and it had run down her cheeks in long, colorful streams. He had never seen her without all of the paint, and was surprised at how beautiful her eyes were naturally.

Unaware of her state, she looked at him very somberly for several moments. "I'm sorry Zidon. Thank you for the offer, but I cannot marry you. I do not love you. Please don't ask me again."

Standing up, she threw a robe around herself and disappeared up the stairs. He sat for a while, wondering if she was going to return from the roof, but eventually gave up. He slowly got dressed, put on his helmet, and headed back to work, sorry that he had told Rahab anything about the Hebrews.

5
WELCOME TO MY TENT

The two men stood outside Joshua's tent, neither of them daring to utter a word. The seconds passed slower than Simeon could ever remember, as he was instantaneously transported back to his childhood. He could vividly recall the tone in his mother's voice, "Just wait until I tell your father what you did." He was again experiencing the feeling of having his stomach tied in a knot, listening through the wall of the family tent as his parents discussed his conduct, and dreading the inevitable.

Overwhelmed with that same childhood emotion, Simeon felt like crying. He just knew Joshua was going to spank him verbally. This was going to hurt in a way much more real and lasting than when his father had spanked him physically as a child.

After what seemed like an eternity of torment, the piece of cloth draped across the front of the tent finally began to move. In the split second before the door was completely opened, Simeon imagined the stern face of his father waiting for him on the other side. When he beheld the kindly smile of the man they met at the campfire, he was momentarily relieved.

The man gestured to Nathan and Simeon saying, "Come in young men, Joshua would like to speak with you." As they stepped toward the tent, Simeon found it odd that the elderly man was so affable considering he was probably ushering them in to be disciplined.

It took a moment for Simeon's eyes to adjust to the candlelight inside the tent. Before he could truly focus, he felt his hand being grasped in a calloused, weathered grip. A loud yet pleasant voice greeted him, "I'm Joshua, welcome to my tent." Neither of the young men could say a word. They were awestruck.

After a pregnant pause, Joshua broke out laughing at their apparent inability to converse. "I've been informed that one of you has quite a tongue, and no problem making himself heard. Yet now I introduce myself, and all you can do is stare?" He laughed again, and this time they relaxed slightly, returning weak smiles.

"So, which one of you defended me this evening?" Joshua inquired. Simeon decided that he might as well own up and get this over with, so he humbly admitted to it. At that, Joshua reached forward and actually embraced him. "Thank you for silencing the murmuring. I'm grateful for your loyalty."

Simeon's mouth hung open, unsure how to respond. He had prepared for a stern rebuke, however was receiving appreciation instead. He was confused, but hoped Joshua couldn't tell.

Desperately attempting to think of something appropriate to say, he blurted out, "Nathan stood by my side." The instant the words left his mouth he groaned. He wanted so much to give Nathan credit, but that remark didn't do him justice. He wished the acknowledgement of his friend would have been more eloquent, but there was no taking it back now.

Joshua replied, "I hear from Caleb that your friend is anxious to battle the Canaanite giants. Is that accurate?"

Nathan found his tongue much faster than Simeon had, "If Adonai is with me, I'll gladly take them on!"

Caleb? Did he say Caleb? Simeon thought. No wonder the stranger at the fire looked so old, it was Caleb, and he *was* older than 60. That morning Simeon wouldn't have believed that by nightfall he'd be in the presence of the two oldest Hebrews in the world. What an amazing turn of events. He felt completely overwhelmed.

Then his next thought turned to his mother. She would have been bitterly disappointed to hear he had entertained Caleb at his fire, and hadn't even offered him a drink of goat's milk. Despite this, he was anxious to get back and tell her he had met both Joshua and Caleb. He quickly decided when he told her, he would leave his lack of hospitality out of the story.

Simeon broke his thoughts about his mother when he noticed Joshua had grown very still, and was studying the two young men before him. Joshua's countenance was reminiscent of Caleb at the fire when Simeon suspected he was praying.

"Are either of you married or betrothed?" Joshua asked after a long silence. A bit shocked, they replied that neither of them were. "Are your families able to take care of themselves?" Both said that they were. "You are both from the tribe of Judah?" Yes, they both were. "What are your names?"

Simeon spoke up first, "I am Simeon, son of Obed, nephew of Nahshon." Seeing approval in Joshua's eyes, he decided right then that he would go wherever Joshua led him without question. Joshua's face wasn't glowing, but it was obvious that he had been in the presence of God. *What more could anyone ask of their leader?* Simeon thought. He was glad he stood up for Joshua, vowing to do so again if faced with the opportunity.

Nathan was quick to follow his friend. "I am Nathan, son of Jonathan, son of Terah." Joshua then looked at Nathan with the same approval he had shown Simeon. From the way Joshua looked Nathan up and down, it appeared he was sizing up Nathan's physical stature.

Joshua's eyes met Nathan's and he chuckled, "I suspect you are pretty good with a sword, young man." Nathan stood a bit taller, stuck out his chest, and announced, "I am in fact, so good that my buddy over there will only wrestle with me now. He cannot stand being bested by my blade."

Joshua's eyes turned to Simeon. "Is this true?" he questioned, smiling widely.

"Well, only partially true," Simeon replied, not wanting to appear inferior. "He is very good with a sword, there is no doubt about that; however, I want to provide him with more of a challenge so he continues to grow as a warrior. There is no opportunity for improvement with the sword, but wrestling challenges him far beyond what he can overcome. He rarely agrees to a match because he knows I'll win."

Joshua threw his head back, letting out a loud, hearty guffaw. It made the others laugh, too.

Simeon was beginning to feel relaxed, and could tell that Nathan was also becoming more comfortable. Briefly allowing his eyes to wander around the tent, he was anxious to see how the famous Joshua lived. He was strangely disappointed, seeing nothing different from his own living quarters. The dishes and blankets were nearly identical to those he had grown up eating from and sleeping under.

He was wondering why he had expected anything different when Joshua asked them if they'd like some fresh goat's milk and manna cakes. They both declined.

Motioning for them to sit with him on a familiar looking blanket in the middle of the tent, Joshua began to explain why Caleb had singled them out. "There is a special, covert assignment, and Adonai has confirmed that you are the two He wants to tackle it. We need you to cross the mountains and the Jordan River. Jericho is the first city on the other side of the river that God has given us. Will you secretly go spy it out?"

There was intense excitement on Joshua's face, and anticipation in his voice as he questioned, "Are you willing to put your lives at risk to do what Adonai has asked of you?"

Simeon knew this was the opportunity to make good on the decision he made a few minutes ago to follow Joshua wherever he led. Turning to Nathan, he could see the thrill on his friend's face. It hadn't taken either of them two seconds to make up their minds. This was the adventure of a lifetime. They would be just like Joshua and Caleb had been 40 years ago, spies sent in to reconnoiter the Promised Land.

The tent filled with two emphatic, booming voices in unison, "Yes!"

+-+-+-+

Every time Rahab refused Zidon's marriage proposals, he got drunk. Today was no exception. Sitting in the street by the idol of Astarte he drank late into the night, crying and begging her for help.

He woke up the next morning, in the street, with his head pounding and his back aching. The other soldiers knew to stay clear of him the day after he had been drinking. Zidon had a foul disposition, and wasn't timid about sharing it with anyone who got in his way.

He was at the palace, waiting impatiently for the king to finish his audience with whoever was in the Royal Assembly Room. Finally, the door opened and Rekem stepped out.

"Hi Zidon. Have you seen Rahab lately?" Rekem asked with his annoying nasal voice. It pierced right to the center of Zidon's aching head, intensifying his discomfort.

"What do you mean by that?" he challenged, getting right in Rekem's face. He was in no mood to hear anything this repulsive man had to say about her.

Backing away and holding his hands up in a sign of surrender, Rekem replied, "Whoa. I didn't mean anything by it. I haven't seen her around, and wondered if everything was okay."

Zidon realized anger only made his head ache worse. He attempted to calm himself as Rekem continued. "Can you believe how many people have found out about the Hebrews? I've never seen so many people so scared. My neighbor actually left town yesterday. He took his whole family to Ai to live with his wife's brother."

Zidon did not answer Rekem; he just rubbed his forehead and eyes hoping for some relief. "You know, you should drink a lot of water. It always helps my head feel better after I've had too much to drink." Zidon glared at Rekem, who quickly scurried down the hallway and out of sight.

6
THE GRAND ADVENTURE

The two young men barely slept that night as they lay in Caleb's tent. They wanted to leave right away and camp under a tree, but Caleb insisted they spend the night and get an early start in the morning.

Simeon lay wide awake, pondering what the next few days might hold. Giants were a scary thought, but he felt certain that Adonai would protect them. He imagined the reception from his parents upon their return from this mission. He could almost feel his mother's warm embrace. The imaginary sight of approval on his father's face nearly made him weep as he rolled over again, trying desperately to get comfortable enough to doze off.

He heard Nathan snoring briefly, but watched him toss and turn most of the night, too. Time crept by as Simeon hoped for sunrise and the start of this quest. Eventually he saw the faintest glimmer of daylight and caught a glimpse of Nathan. His eyes were wide open, too. They grinned at each other and wasted little time on preparations for the journey.

After a hearty breakfast of manna cakes and goat's milk, they were ascending Mount Nebo before the sun was fully visible in the sky.

Given only rudimentary instructions as to which way to go, and what to look for when they got to Jericho, they had even less information on how to keep from being discovered. Joshua was, however, thorough in impressing on them the necessity for absolute secrecy. He wouldn't even allow them to go back to their families, but sent a messenger to explain they would be gone for a while.

As Nathan and Simeon descended the backside of Mount Nebo, they chattered excitedly about seeing the largest city either of them would ever have encountered. What an exhilarating change this would be from their boring desert routine. There was animated discussion about what it would be like to eat their food, sleep inside a walled city, interact with the people, what the women might look like, and what a grand adventure this would be. Both were living out a childhood fantasy to be one of the spies sent into Canaan, and each was determined to bring back God's report, not his own.

Caught up in speculation, the men barely noticed their surroundings as they approached the Jordan River. Their optimism lapsed, if only briefly. It was flood season, and the muddy, fast moving water was overflowing its banks with fury. They stood for a while discussing a plan to somehow ford the bursting waterway and were growing discouraged, when several foreigners came along with camels, headed upriver.

The men scoffed at them and informed Simeon and Nathan that there was no way any man or beast could cross this river for a significant distance in either direction. "We'd like to stay and watch, if you are going to give it a try!" one teased with his strong accent as they all laughed uproariously.

Rather than entertain the travelers and be swept away in the torrent, Simeon and Nathan decided it would be best to join the caravan. They enjoyed the company of the voyagers as they traveled upstream to a place where it was safe to attempt to ford the swollen river.

The kindly wayfarers helped them navigate the river on the backs of their heavily laden camels, and were amused by the Hebrews' lack of experience with the ungraceful, homely, and temperamental animals.

Significantly off course and behind schedule, Simeon and Nathan knew the general direction toward Jericho and picked up their pace. As the orange glow of the sun disappeared over the horizon, their stomachs were gnawing at them. The manna they had gathered before leaving camp that morning was gratefully consumed. They knew there would be no manna on this side of the Jordan in the morning. Instead of being concerned about this, they had both been daydreaming about what kinds of food they would encounter in Jericho.

There was a slight chill in the air, but it was warm enough that they didn't need to build a fire. Finding large, smooth stones from the riverbank on which to rest their heads, they laid down in a meadow of tall green grass near a grove of trees.

Simeon enjoyed the sounds of the insects darting about, as he lay awake, gazing at the stars. He listened to their buzzing interaction for quite a while. Eventually, he figured Nathan was asleep and dreaming of what heroes they'd be, but his own thoughts weren't so carefree.

He wondered how many of the men were giving his father grief for the disrespectful actions of his son. He hoped they hadn't been harsh with Obed, since it wasn't his fault. He rehearsed the exact wording of how he'd phrase the apology to his father, but decided no matter what, he would not repent to anyone for his words, only for the fact that they were spoken to his elders. The sentiment was justified. Even Joshua approved of what he said, and he found comfort in that.

Simeon drifted off to sleep and dreamed of toothless old men taking his father's shoe, the ultimate sign of disgrace, as they walked past him. Somehow in his dream, Obed always had another shoe to give the next man. The line to humiliate him seemed to have no end.

The next thing Simeon knew, Nathan was tapping him on the shoulder telling him to wake up. They had been so tired from the nearly sleepless night in Caleb's tent that they overslept this morning. The sun was well into the sky. They needed to get moving.

As they trudged toward Jericho, they were each caught up in their own thoughts. *What if the inhabitants really are giants, and they find out what we are up to? What if we never get to see our families again? What if I don't get to make things right with my father?*

Nathan broke into Simeon's thoughts, "Do you remember when Adonai made His covenant with Father Abraham?"

What a silly question, Simeon thought. *Every good Hebrew knows that story forward and backward. We heard it at least once a week as children. It was that covenant that gave us hope as slaves in Egypt.*

Assuming this was more than just an academic inquiry, he guardedly responded, "Sure, I remember it," and then added, "Why?"

"Well, I was thinking about what Adonai said to Abraham about how we would come back to the land, but not until..." at this point, Nathan paused, waiting for Simeon to complete the phrase.

His eyes grew huge as he added, "..until the iniquity of the Amorites is complete." Oh my!

Simeon's mind was racing. What might that phrase mean? He had heard it hundreds of times, but never thought about how those words might affect him personally.

His stomach was sinking further and further as he now imagined, with a whole new perspective, what Jericho might be like. If their iniquity was finally "complete," the Promised Land must be a terribly evil place. If they had gotten so bad that now God was ready to judge them and take away their land, they must be a very corrupt people indeed. He wasn't so excited about eating their food, sleeping in a walled city, or meeting their women anymore.

Nathan broke into Simeon's thoughts again with the quiet announcement, "I can see the wall."

Simeon was almost afraid to look, because he knew it meant there was no getting out of their mission; nevertheless, he raised his eyes from the dirt in front of him to get his first glimpse of this iniquitous place.

7
A GRAVE SITUATION

The walls were even taller than he had expected. The obvious concern on Nathan's face confirmed that neither of them was thinking of it as a grand adventure at this particular moment.

They had agreed earlier to not split up, but to scout it out together, so they headed around the outside of the city to find the gate. The gravity of their situation was weighing heavily on Simeon. He stared straight ahead, his brow deeply furrowed. He spotted something lying near the wall, but did not point it out to Nathan. The closer they got, the more convinced he became that it was a dead body. Eventually, the stench confirmed his fears, and alerted Nathan to its presence.

He tried not to look at it as they approached, but could not help but sneak a glance. He wished at once that he hadn't done so. There were two decomposing bodies, not just one. He wondered what they had done, and why no one had taken the time to bury them.

The horrifying sight was seared into his mind. Fear gripped him, but he tried to shake it off. They were now very near the city gate. He was attempting to take mental notes about how tall, how many guards, and such, but was distracted by the discovery of windows built right into the wall all around Jericho, with no apparent pattern as to their placement.

These windows temporarily took his mind off of the unwelcome thoughts. Simeon wondered what it would be like to live in a house adjoining the wall of a great city, with a window to see what was happening outside. He decided he would one day enjoy those circumstances.

A few steps beyond the entrance of Jericho, Simeon realized they hadn't discussed a plan for once they arrived. Rather than attract attention by stopping Nathan, they moved along in silence.

After a few seconds, he also realized it was a moot point; they were already garnering plenty of curiosity. Their drab, ill-fitting, worn desert clothing and sandals did not blend in with the fine city wear of the people eyeing them suspiciously.

Nathan attempted to muster a smile, but instead looked like a frightened child. The further into the city they walked, the darker it felt. Although he was desperately trying to avoid eye contact, one man caught and held Simeon's gaze long enough for him to determine that the people fearfully staring at them had no light in their eyes.

He was also troubled to observe that some of them were truly giants. Simeon was relatively tall amongst his own people, but here, he felt like a grasshopper, and instantly understood why the ten spies had chosen that terminology.

To his left, he noticed what appeared to be a slave auction, but was dismayed by the fact that the slaves for sale were small children; mostly girls.

His eyes wandered from there and lit on a corner with two heavily painted harlots fighting over a filthy looking man. His toothless smile and loud laugh were proof that he was heartily enjoying their battle over him.

Simeon's stomach sank as he noticed several drunk people were stumbling around celebrating underneath a row of gallows that had recently been put to use. Their victims were dangling high above the street, as the breeze caused them to sway back and forth.

He looked past all of this and noticed a soldier walking up a side street. He approached a man, pulled out his sword, stabbed the man, then walked away as if nothing had happened. Others watched it happen with disturbing disinterest.

As fear tightened its grip on Simeon, he wished with all his heart that he were back in his tent, with none of these surreal mental pictures to plague him.

As they passed throngs of curious onlookers, Simeon could hear voices whispering excitedly behind them. Although neither of them knew where they were headed, they continued moving without a word. Simeon felt sick to his stomach, and longed for some fresh air to clear his senses. He had never imagined a people as wicked as these.

Out of the corner of his eye, Simeon caught a glimpse of several soldiers who were observing them with concern on their faces. One was smaller framed, with shifty eyes. Simeon looked at the group of men long enough to realize that this devious looking man was actually taller than Nathan. However, compared to the other soldiers, he looked small. He gave a panicked order, and two of them ran in opposite directions.

Fear gripped Simeon. Apparently aware of the two spies, the oversized soldiers were summoning more troops.

Simeon grabbed Nathan by the tunic, tugging violently, "We've got to get out of here, now!" He dragged Nathan down a side street. They began to move faster, nearly running, randomly turning this way and that, without direction.

Suddenly, a small, thin, heavily painted woman was standing directly in front of them. Surprisingly, she didn't appear to be in any hurry to move out of their way. Startled by her boldness, they froze and stared at her while she curiously studied them. Her eyes travelled discerningly from the top their heads to the shoes on their feet. She flatly issued the command, "Come with me," and turned down another side street, quickly moving away from the crowds amassing behind the two "strangers."

Simeon and Nathan had to hustle to keep from losing sight of the nimble woman who was whisking them away. He wondered why they had blindly obeyed her order, why his stomach wasn't in knots like it had been only a couple of minutes before, and why he was strangely filled with peace despite their circumstances.

They practically ran as she led them through a maze of city streets lined with houses, merchants, and altars. Simeon was dismayed to pass shrines and "holy places" at nearly every turn with statues of pagan gods of varying size and shape. Once again, he felt sick to his stomach, sensing the overwhelming evil in Jericho.

He specifically noticed one idol that looked like a haughty man with a very tall, conical hat. He had a sword in one hand and a lightning bolt in the other. Simeon wondered if this was the "moon god" that the city was named after.

Several corners later another statue caught and held his attention. It appeared to be bronze, and was a woman wearing nothing but a horned headdress and pearls. She held a lily in one hand and a serpent in the other. Knowing how Adonai felt about modesty, Simeon resisted the temptation to stop hustling and take a closer look at her unclothed body. He wondered what Nathan was thinking of this disgusting city.

As they continued through the streets, he became more and more distressed about the state of these pagan people, and pondered what would induce them to worship these silent "gods" that were fashioned by human hands.

He observed that some of the idols had incense burning near them, while others were caked in dried blood. All of them looked sinister to him, and he had a better understanding of why God had decided to destroy these people. He was beginning to grasp the statement "their iniquity is complete."

They had climbed a few stairs along the way, and he was irrevocably lost. He hoped Nathan's sense of direction was more reliable than his own, so they could navigate back out of this labyrinth.

The woman disappeared into a doorway, motioning for the men to join her. With little more than a moment of hesitation, and a brief opportunity to glance backward at the crowd still following them from a distance, they ducked through the door without an idea of what awaited them there. For several moments, they were nearly blind in the relative darkness of the house, until their eyes adjusted to the dim lighting.

She motioned for them to sit against the wall, put her finger to her lips and said, "Ssh" quietly. Since neither of them could grasp what had just happened, where they were, or why this woman had taken them in, they were obedient and sat motionless.

She stood at the door frowning for quite a while, straining to hear what was happening outside. There was total silence and no communication for so long that it began to grow dark outside. Simeon wanted desperately to peek out the window behind and above him to see what was happening in the street, but could tell by her manner that things weren't going well on the other side of the door.

Suddenly, struck with panic, she whispered loudly to them, "Quickly, follow me to the roof. You can hide there." She headed up, not waiting for a response. They followed, crested the stairs, and found themselves on a flat roof. "Here are some stalks of flax, use them to cover yourselves. Be completely silent, and I will tell them you have gone." With that command, she disappeared back down the stairs.

+-+-+-+

Zidon was standing near the King who was instructing several men about the preparations for the New Year Festival. It was the biggest, rowdiest, most drunken festival of the year for the people of Jericho, and the King wanted this upcoming one to be the best ever.

Zidon felt honored to have been chosen to head the detail in charge of food and wine for the festival. He was caught up in his own thoughts about Rahab, and unable to keep his mind focused on what the king was telling the other men. If only he could swallow his pride, forgive her rejection, and go tell her about his new appointment. Surely she would be happy for him.

His mind was dragged back to the palace by a commotion at the door. Zidon could hear someone saying, "But I was told to alert the King at once. You must let me speak with him." Eventually the palace guards gave in. Opening the chamber doors, one of them reluctantly announced, "Rekem is here to see you, my lord."

"Let the little weasel in," the King replied without looking up from the tablet in his hands.

"My lord, oh most holy King, ruler of Jericho, your humble servant begs your forgiveness for this intrusion."

"Just say what you want, Rekem." The King replied, not at all impressed with his groveling.

"Oh most gracious King, there are two men. They are inside Jericho right now. They look as though they might have come from the desert, and are here to spy on us."

The King jumped up as though he had been struck with lightning. He began giving orders to everyone he could see. "You! Shut the gate. You! Post guards. You! Alert the soldiers. You!" he turned and looked at Zidon, "Find me those men!"

Zidon nearly ran from the palace. He didn't even know where to begin looking for them. He started asking the people on the street. Some said they knew nothing of any desert people, and others, with fear in their eyes, went into vivid detail about how the men had looked.

He followed the pointed fingers across town, up that street, around this corner, down that alley, up those stairs. Finally he found one beggar man who seemed as though he actually knew what he was talking about. He said that they had gone into a woman's house.

"Can you show me that house?" Zidon asked him. "Certainly." Came the reply.

"Take me there now. There isn't any time to lose." Zidon commanded him.

The old beggar took him directly to the street on which Rahab lived. As they walked past the neighboring doors, Zidon almost told the man to stop; he didn't want to know where they went. He had a sinking feeling that he knew exactly where they ended up.

Don't be jealous, this is her livelihood. She has never been one to turn away business, especially from travelers with lots of money. He was reasoning with himself as they drew nearer. You have no right to get upset with her for taking them in.

The beggar man stopped directly in front of her door, pointed, and said, "This is the house they went into. I'm certain of it." Zidon ordered the beggar not to tell anyone else where they went, and sent him away without so much as a "thank you."

He stood in the street looking at her door for quite some time before working up the courage to knock. Usually he was so excited to see her that he would nearly rattle things off her wall with the vigor behind his knuckles. Today, he was surprised she even heard his faint rapping on the door.

She quickly opened the door as if she knew who it was. This puzzled him, but he knew he had ugly business that needed to be addressed and pushed that thought aside. They hadn't spoken since their last uncomfortable parting. He was still hurt by her unwavering refusal.

"Where are the two spies?" he asked without even a greeting.

"Spies? I don't know what you are talking about," came the terse reply.

He couldn't stand to be short with her, and quickly decided to change his approach. His voice softened a bit, "Rahab, the townspeople saw two desert men come into your house. I'm not upset with you; I just need you to bring them out. They are here to spy out this country."

"Oh, the desert men. Yes, they did come here, but they already left." She didn't even look at Zidon as she spoke. He assumed she was still upset about their last meeting, too.

"Who were they? Why were they here? Where were they going?" he asked without pausing between inquiries.

"I don't know. I don't ask questions. They were here. They left just as the gates were being closed. If you hurry you can probably catch them and ask whatever questions you want in person. Sorry, I cannot help you. Goodbye, Zidon."

She started to close the door. Zidon couldn't bear to part this way, so he put his hand in the way and opened it back up. The resolute look in Rahab's eyes had him at a loss for words.

The two of them stood in silence staring at each other, both with distressed looks on their faces. Finally Rahab turned away and this time Zidon let her close the door.

8
THE PAGAN WOMAN

On this strange woman's roof, Simeon and Nathan exchanged a nervous glance, and did their best to quietly cover themselves with the long stalks. Before they had completely "settled in," she was back. There was deep concern on her face as she sat down beside them and spoke quietly but intensely.

"I know your God has given you this land. We are all terrified of you. All the inhabitants are fainthearted because of you. We have heard how Adonai dried up the water of the Red Sea for you when your people came out of Egypt. We have heard what you did to the two kings of the Amorites, Sihon and Og, on the other side of the Jordan River, how you totally destroyed them."

Simeon could barely believe his ears. This woman, this pagan, Canaanite woman, this enemy of the Hebrews who was hiding them from the townspeople, this woman knew of Adonai? She knew of Moses? She knew of their escape from slavery and recent victories?

She continued, "As soon as we heard these things, our hearts melted. Our courage failed us because of you. Adonai, your God, He is God in heaven above and on earth beneath."

Simeon's mouth was now literally hanging open in shock. This pagan woman who lived in a city named "The House of the Moon God," who daily passed altars to Ba'al and every other pagan god imaginable, was admitting that Adonai is indeed God of everything? How did she know of Him? Where did she get this amazing faith in the midst of such a culture?

"Now, therefore I beg you, swear to me by Adonai, since I have shown you kindness, that you will also show kindness to my father's house. Please give me your word that you will spare my father, mother, brothers and sisters, and all that they have." She was now pleading with them. "Swear to me that you will deliver our lives from death!"

Simeon's mind was still reeling from the shock of all that she had just said. Finally, he spoke the first words either of them had uttered since seeing the soldiers in the street. "Our lives for yours. None of you tell this business of ours to anyone. When the Lord has given us this land, we will deal kindly and truly with you."

The woman, visibly relieved by his oath, actually smiled at them. Then, she stiffened as though she heard something, got up, and motioned for them to follow her once again. As they went back down into her house, she informed them she had sent the soldiers out of the city gate to pursue them to the Jordan. The gates were now barricaded, so it was impossible for them to retreat by that venue. "Get to the mountain, lest they meet you. Hide in the mountains three days; until the pursuers have returned. After that, you may go your way."

While disclosing her deception, she had retrieved a scarlet colored rope and was tying it to the large wooden table in the center of the room. It was then that Simeon ascertained they were in one of the houses that actually adjoined the wall with a window looking out through it.

He had been so eager to experience a house with a window in the wall. Now, here he was, and he was extremely anxious to get out. If the situation weren't so grave, he might have laughed at the irony of it.

Preparing to descend through the window, Simeon said, "We will only honor this oath we have made to you if, when we return to this land, you bind this scarlet rope in the window you are letting us down through. You must have your father, mother, brothers, and your father's entire household in this house with you.

Whoever goes outside the doors of your house into the street, his blood will be on his own head, and we will be guiltless. Whoever is with you in your house, his blood will be on our head if a hand is laid on him." He then reiterated the condition of this pact, "However, if you tell this business of ours to anyone, we will be free of this oath which you made us swear."

While Simeon was still speaking, Nathan squeezed his stocky frame out of the window, and was safely on the ground almost immediately. Simeon followed, and as his sandals quickly touched the gravel, he realized her window was not very far above his head. They were not as high as he had imagined. The wall rose quite far above the level of her roof.

She poked her head partially out of the window, whispering loudly, "According to your words, so be it." Pointing in the direction they were to go, she motioned her hands in a shooing fashion telling them to leave. Her head disappeared back into the window, and she was gone.

The two nervous young men crouched perfectly still for a few moments, straining to hear footsteps approaching, but heard none. Without a word, they headed in the direction the mysterious woman had indicated. Simeon was unconcerned that she might be sending them into a trap, just as he had no fear as she commanded them to follow her in the city.

Grateful for the moonlight to guide them, they cautiously climbed further and further from Jericho. Simeon could see in the faint, silvery light that the steep cliffs she had pointed toward were dotted with caves.

After scaling the rocky mountainside investigating each chamber, they finally found a cavern large enough for both of them near the top of the cliff. Attempting to get comfortable in the extremely tight space, they made camp for what remained of the night.

Simeon whispered in Nathan's ear to go to sleep, he'd take the first watch. Nodding his head, Nathan leaned back against the cold, damp wall. After quite a while, Simeon could hear his breathing slow and get deeper. He was grateful that his friend was resting.

The minutes crept by as Simeon replayed the day's sordid events, from their first glimpse of the intimidating city wall, to their last view shortly after leaving the painted woman's house earlier that evening.

He questioned why they hadn't devised a plan for once they reached the city. He despaired over the report they would have to give Joshua regarding their secret mission. He was amazed at how they managed to run right into a woman who believed in, and what's more, trusted Adonai. He imagined what had taken place downstairs while they were hiding under flax stalks on her roof. He pondered what her name might be, and why they hadn't thought to ask. And again, he dreaded what they were going to tell Joshua.

Simeon realized Joshua would be profoundly disappointed in them. Not only did they bind themselves by oath to a pagan woman, but there was a serious lack of viable information gathered during this venture. They knew very little more about Jericho than they had that same morning, and there was certainly no hope of returning to investigate further.

He thought carefully about what he would advise Joshua, if he were asked, about how and where to attack the city. After much deliberation, considering the lack of usable facts, he was dismayed to admit that it might be best to hope they could gain access through the gate somehow. *What a pitiful plan*, he thought.

Time continued to creep by, and Simeon was unsure how long he had been lost in thought, but his eyelids began to grow heavy. He stood, bumping his head against the low hanging roof, and cautiously attempted to move around a bit. His head throbbed, so he sat back down. His mind drifted to his father, and what he would tell Obed about their "grand adventure."

Well, Father, Joshua commissioned Nathan and me for a secret spy mission to reconnoiter the land. We traveled to Jericho by way of a lengthy detour. Upon arriving, we got hopelessly lost in the city, until a pagan woman invited us into her house. We spent the day there, hid on the roof like cowards, promised to spare her life, sneaked out through a window, and concealed ourselves in a cave on a mountain for three days afterward.

We discovered nothing about their military capabilities, the layout of the city, or their procedures regarding the city gate. We were unable to observe when they open and close it, how closely it is guarded, or even how thick it is. Realistically, we learned absolutely nothing of military importance.

There is, however, some good news. The pagan woman assured us that the people, who really are giants, are all scared of us. Isn't that great? Aren't you proud of me?

Simeon almost laughed out loud at the notion of recounting it in that manner to his father. He might have found some humor, if it weren't so pathetic. As depression began to set in, he decided it was Nathan's turn to keep watch.

He quietly woke his friend, who took a moment to get his bearings and signaled it was okay for Simeon to go to sleep. He laid down best he could in the cramped space, and closed his eyes, saying a quick prayer that Nathan would be able to stay awake.

He expected to fall asleep quickly, and could have drifted off easily a few minutes ago, but as he prayed for Nathan, he thought about how it would be without a father to regale with tales of their spying adventure.

Nathan's father Jonathan, barely twenty when God proclaimed His judgment, had died several years ago. His mother had been only fourteen when they were married, a few months after the death sentence. They tried not to have children, out of concern for how she would provide for them after he passed away, however, God chose to bless them with three sons and one daughter.

Every evening for over thirty years, Nathan's parents voiced their love for each other, and each child received an embrace and a spoken blessing, in case Jonathan didn't wake up in the morning. Every morning for nearly forty years, he woke up and was thrilled to have another day to spend with his family. Simeon envied the unbounded affection and acceptance Nathan had received from his father, something Simeon had not experienced.

Eventually sleep overcame him, and he drifted off, wishing he'd wake up in his own tent, with all of this having been only a dream.

+-+-+-+

Zidon had taken it on himself to head the search party that went looking for the two desert travelers. He hadn't even returned to the palace to share the depressing news with the

King. His time was better spent rounding up the sneakiest men he could find on such short notice. He was able to locate Rekem, who was only too eager to join such a mission.

The King had called him a "weasel" for good reason. If there was dirty work to be done, he was always the first to volunteer. It didn't hurt that he knew the King was generous with rewards for valuable information.

Zidon wasn't exactly happy to spend his time with Rekem, so he split the men into two search parties. Rekem took only two men and went to the mountains to search the caves. Zidon wanted to head the larger party that went to the Jordan.

Although nobody was sure that these two men were Hebrews, Zidon knew that if they were, they would have to cross the Jordan somewhere in order to return to their people.

The band of searching soldiers spent three days looking everywhere between Jericho and the Jordan River. They tried to find any sign of the two men, but were unable. Zidon was bitterly disappointed by their lack of success.

The third evening, he had to agree with his men that the spies had either evaded them quite expertly, or had left the city in a different direction.

Returning to Jericho, Zidon hoped that Rekem had been successful, but was afraid that he would have to admit defeat to the King. This was territory he was unfamiliar with. He had risen in the ranks of soldiers due to his overwhelming tenacity. He had never known defeat in battle, and was very proud of his fighting record.

Nearing the wall surrounding Jericho, he surveyed it with a different outlook. He even stopped walking to study it from the perspective of the captain of the Hebrew army.

He thought about how he would try to take the city with nearly unlimited manpower. The gate seemed the obvious weak point. It was made of thick wood, not solid stone like the rest of the wall, and once breached, ladders would not be necessary for the Hebrew soldiers to literally pour into the city. Zidon decided if he were attacking, he would concentrate his efforts there.

"If only we would have caught those two spies!" He lamented aloud. The evasive Hebrew visitors were making him look bad to the King, and that deed certainly could not go unpunished.

Zidon hoped his chance to get revenge would come soon. *If it takes until my dying breath*, he silently vowed, *I will find those two men and make them pay. They have destroyed my hard earned reputation for success.*

9
A GOD KIND OF MIRACLE

The three days in that cave were the longest Simeon had ever experienced. The first afternoon they could hear Jericho soldiers climbing around on the ledges below them, checking the other caves. As night fell, he knew they'd be back in the morning, ascending higher, and discovering their hiding place.

Simeon was sure they had climbed as high as was possible on the side of the mountain. There was nowhere else for them to go but back down toward Jericho, and that certainly wasn't an option. There would definitely be guards posted to watch for any movement. They could not possibly scale the rocky mountainside without being detected. They had to stay where they were. Nothing but a miracle could help them now.

Simeon prayed more fervently that evening than ever before. "Please send us a diversion," he pleaded. "Please send us a deliverer, or a way to hide. Please don't let your servants die, or worse yet, be captured!"

Keeping guard that night, Simeon expected something big to happen in response to his prayers. "A torrential rainstorm would keep the soldiers off the cliffs," he respectfully advised God. "Thunder and lightning would be a nice, dramatic touch," he added. "You know, some intense wind would make them think twice about climbing this high." The ideas continued long into the darkness of the night, but those were the two recommendations he felt were most probable to succeed.

As the hours dragged on, he heard no rain, no wind, and no thunder. Aside from the sound of bugs flitting around in the moonlight, it was still and silent outside the cave.

Simeon began to get upset. He was so filled with faith earlier, but the longer he waited to see God move, the more disappointed he became. "Adonai, you could part the Red Sea for the children of Israel. Why can't you keep the soldiers away from this one cave?"

In the moonlight illuminating the mouth of the cave, Simeon strained his eyes to see anything God might be doing to help them. Even though he stared out for a long time, he saw nothing but a small spider hanging near the top of the entrance.

As he prepared to go kill it, he paused - deciding they were both in similar situations that night. The spider was living a short, meaningless life, and it was about to be snuffed out by someone who didn't care. There was no one to come to its rescue. Simeon's life was soon to be taken by a pagan soldier, and there was nothing he could do to stop the inevitable event.

In his anger toward God, he stood too quickly, hit his head, kicked the rock wall, and sat back down pouting. He decided the insignificant spider wasn't worth the effort and instead took some of his frustration out on Nathan's shoulder. Simeon shook him rather violently, alerting him that it was his turn to keep guard.

The next morning he was awakened by strange voices nearby. Apparently Nathan had fallen asleep and was also startled awake by the soldiers outside.

Sitting perfectly still, the only sound Simeon could hear was the terribly loud beating of his heart, which had somehow migrated up into his throat.

His mind was racing. *What do we do once they get to our cave? Do we jump out and try to escape? How many soldiers are there? If there are only a couple, we could surprise, and probably defeat them. What if there are too many? Do we just go with them peacefully? Do pagans practice torture?*

These thoughts, flying through his head, were interrupted by a shadow across the mouth of the cave. He heard the gruff voice say, "Hey, Rekem, come look at this spider web. It covers the whole doorway!"

Simeon looked at Nathan, who had panic on his face. He hoped his friend would be able to get a sword away from one of the soldiers and put it to good use in their defense.

"Let's keep moving. Did you check all of the caves on this side?" called out another voice, much more nasal sounding. "We can't afford to lose any time admiring nature in the door of an obviously empty cave. We've got spies to find. Get moving NOW!"

Within a couple of moments Simeon could hear the soldiers moving away from their cave. Suddenly, it was totally silent inside the cave and out.

Simeon didn't know what to think. The very last thing he remembered from the night before was his disappointment with God, and the decision to not get up and kill that spider. Relief swept over him in a wave, and he fought back tears.

He got down on his knees, closed his eyes, gave way to the tears, and repented for his unbelief. Gratitude overwhelmed him as he thanked Adonai with every fiber of his being. God had placed that tiny bug there for their protection. The concept was mind-blowing. He expected some kind of "thunder-and-lightning" miracle, but got a silent, small miracle instead.

The following morning, as they broke through the web to leave the cave and sneak back across the Jordan, Simeon looked for the spider that had spun such a large web in such a short time. He felt as though he ought to thank the tiny creature for saving their lives. He questioned whether it had spent all its allotted energy, and therefore it's very life, spinning that web in a single night.

Unfortunately, he could not find the spider anywhere near the cave, and wondered sadly if one of the soldiers had killed it.

+-+-+-+

Zidon and his search party made their way around to the tightly locked city gate. He called an order out to the guard, a young man whom he did not recognize. The guard ignored him.

"In the name of the King, I order you to open this gate!"

About that time, Rekem poked his head above the wall and told the young man that he should indeed open the gate immediately. This was the search party they were waiting for.

"I want the name of that guard!" Zidon's voice boomed out.

"Relax; he's merely a boy, doing what he was told to do." Rekem replied. "The King has given strict orders that no one comes in, and no one goes out. How was he to know that you were the one exception to that order?"

Deciding not to press the issue, he asked Rekem, "so, did you find the spies?"

"Nah. They weren't in the caves. I don't think anyone really expected them to take to the mountains, anyway. They must have just been way too fast for us, and crossed the Jordan before we got there." Rekem didn't seem bothered at all by the fact that he had failed in his mission to retrieve the two men.

Zidon thought even less of Rekem than he did before. Rekem was such a slimy man, Zidon decided he wouldn't be surprised if Rekem switched allegiances if the Hebrews did attack.

"How is the King taking all of this?" Zidon inquired as they walked toward the palace.

"If you ask me, he's shaking in his boots. He's ordered all of the people to offer double sacrifices to their gods, and he's commissioned a larger statue of Ba'al to be cast immediately. Apparently, the smaller ones in town are insufficient. He wants everyone to know who protects Jericho from foreign soldiers."

Zidon shook his head as they approached the palace gates. He didn't want to face the King, but knew it was inevitable. Drawing some extra courage from deep inside himself, he told the guards to announce their return.

+-+-+-+

Nathan and Simeon's insides gnawed at them as they left the cave, descended the mountain, and proceeded toward the Israelite camp. The manna provisions had been consumed the first day, and they were very hungry.

They had expected to spend maybe one day in the city, scout it out, eat local food, and camp out by a creek on their way back. Manna was the only food to take with them from camp, and except on the Sabbath, it always rotted by the second morning.

The rocky cliff that had been their temporary housing didn't support any edible plant life, but they obtained fresh water from the dripping overflow of a small spring along the top near their cave.

Simeon had not planned to be in enemy territory for longer than one day, nor had he expected to be in hiding where he could not even stand up straight. Three days of near total silence and very little sleep, combined with intense hunger and achy backs, had left them both short-tempered.

As they descended the mountain, Nathan accidentally slipped, dislodging a boulder, which crashed into Simeon's calf. The same sharp stone had injured both young men, however, Simeon responded with an uncharacteristic scowl. A loudly whispered chastisement expressed his pent up frustration. Nathan's silence for the rest of the journey caused Simeon to regret that he had spoken so harshly.

Cresting Mount Nebo, Simeon was surprised to observe that the Children of Israel were making preparations to relocate the camp. Nathan was surely intrigued also, but neither of them said anything about it; they just continued to walk toward Joshua's tent. Nobody paid any attention to them, and they didn't dare ask anyone where they might find Joshua or Caleb, for fear of attracting curiosity. As they made their way through the teeming crowd, they sensed excitement in the air. Some people appeared downright giddy.

"Simeon! Nathan! Over here!" a voice called out. They turned to see Caleb's smiling face as he beckoned them. Simeon had already decided what he was going to tell Joshua, but due to the required silence while hiding out, the two men had not spoken about it with each other.

Joshua embraced them both, grateful to see them again. He looked at them with his brow furrowed, "You look like you have not slept in days."

Nathan spoke up and said, "We're okay, but we could sure use something to eat, if you don't mind."

With that, Joshua motioned to another man standing behind them, who returned quickly with cakes and milk. In all his life, Simeon never could recall anyone cooking manna in a way that tasted so good, and the goat was surely blessed in a special way, as her milk was the richest he'd ever had.

With food in their bellies, the two of them started to perk up. The situation didn't look as dreary and grim as it had on their walk back from the mountain. Joshua had gone off to make some more preparations, and left the two friends alone to eat. Finally, Nathan broke the silence, "So, are we going to give Joshua a good report?"

Simeon looked at his friend, who had a twinkle in his eye, and was fighting back a smile. "Is there any other report to give?" He responded, still angry with himself about the incident with the boulder. Nathan was determined, "How much of it should we tell him? Does he need to know that we had no plan once we entered Jericho? Should we explain how we had to have a pagan woman hide us from their soldiers?" By now he was fully smiling, and taunting Simeon with his playful words.

After a long pause, Simeon laughed at the absurdity of the situation. They hadn't had a plan, and they did hide like cowards, but it sounded so much worse than it had actually been.

Before he could formulate a witty answer, Joshua and Caleb returned with about a dozen other men who all crowded into the tent. He introduced them as his military commanders, the men who were responsible for each tribe. They were here for the briefing about how to take Jericho.

Simeon recognized only one of them, his cousin Salmon, the son of his father's uncle, Nahshon. He was a prince among the tribe of Judah. Simeon figured if he was here to represent Judah, then the other men had to be at least as important within their own tribes.

Joshua then addressed the group of men. "The morning we began making preparations to move, I sent these two young men to spy out Jericho and the surrounding land. They returned a few minutes ago, and are now fed and ready to share what they discovered." He looked at Simeon and Nathan with expectation on his face at what the two friends were about to tell all of them.

There was an uncomfortable silence for a few moments as Simeon and Nathan looked at each other wide-eyed. Not only did they not want to confess to Joshua that they had very little information, but now they had to admit it to all of his military commanders as well. The only thing that could make this worse would be if his father were present to witness the humiliation. Simeon wished he hadn't eaten so much manna. His stomach wasn't very happy with him at that moment.

After what felt like an eternity, Nathan cleared his throat, stood to his feet, and turned to address the group of men. "Truly Adonai has delivered the land into our hands. All of the inhabitants are in fear of us, and have become fainthearted."

With this announcement, the men threw their hands in the air and cheered. They hugged each other, hugged Joshua and Caleb, and hugged the two young men. Simeon thought he even saw tears in Caleb's eyes.

Simeon was shocked at their response. These military men had not required any specifics from them before they trusted Adonai for a victory. Maybe the children of Israel had actually learned their lesson, and had come to a point where they knew God could indeed give them a victory. The thought thrilled him to his very core.

The celebration continued until Joshua sent the men home. He cautioned them not to tell anyone about the spies or about what they had heard. He stressed that the time was not yet at hand for the congregation to be informed about it. He kept Salmon for a few extra moments, taking him aside and speaking with him alone.

When it was just the four of them again, Joshua and Caleb sat down, asking for more information on what had happened. Simeon was grateful he had the other men leave before making them admit the rest of their story.

As they began relating to Joshua and Caleb the dreary details of their few minutes of actual spying, the two of them exchanged concerned glances repeatedly. When Nathan admitted they had bound themselves by an oath to the pagan woman, Caleb actually stood up and began pacing back and forth.

They finished their story with the three days in the cave.

When Simeon got to the part about the spider, he saw Joshua's frown begin to change.

Simeon apologized for the lack of actual reconnaissance gathered on their trip. They both felt badly that they couldn't offer more information that would be instrumental in the battle plan.

At this, Joshua finally spoke up. "I must admit, Adonai has not given me a battle plan yet. I had hoped that the two of you would find their weak spot, a place where we could focus our attack. I suspect He is asking me to trust Him, and not make my own plan, just like He expected you to trust Him in the cave.

"The fact that the people are afraid of us may indeed prove to be very helpful. I am grateful that you were able to gather that much information, and amazed at how God used a pagan…" he smiled at them and continued, "and a spider to protect you from the soldiers. He works in mysterious ways."

By this time, the sun had gone down. Joshua said to the young men, "I can see you are very tired. Your return trip must have been a difficult one." He directed them to Caleb's tent, and told them to be ready to move out first thing in the morning.

"I don't mean to sound ungrateful for the invitation," Simeon replied as they rose to their feet, "but may I just go home and sleep there?"

Joshua walked over, gently placing his hand on Simeon's shoulder. "Simeon, we need to keep the trip to Jericho as quiet as possible. If you return to your families, it will create too much speculation. It would be best if you remain with us until we have arrived in the Promised Land and Jericho has been taken. Your parents will be informed of your safe return."

Simeon and Nathan lay down in the same places they had the night before they left. Simeon thought for a few moments about how it seemed like much longer than it had actually been. He was incredibly tired and had no problem falling asleep.

10
EXCITEMENT IN THE AIR

It seemed but a few moments, and Caleb was shaking Simeon's shoulder telling him it was time to get up. Opening his eyes, he stretched and saw Nathan was also waking up. The sun was already high in the sky, and Caleb needed to get his tent packed up. It was time to move out. The two of them had slept soundly for many hours longer than everyone else. Joshua had been up since the break of dawn, and almost everyone was ready to move out.

The Hebrew people had honed the moving routine to a science, having done it so many times in their lives. Everyone knew his job; nobody sat around. They knew how to pack things and how to travel well.

Simeon and Nathan helped the others take Caleb's tent down and pack it for transport. The excitement in the air was contagious. Caught up in the songs people were singing, Simeon felt quite at home, although his family's tent was far on the other side of the camp and he didn't recognize a single face.

Wondering again what Joshua had told his family, he hoped his siblings were doing well at taking over his duties. He knew that his father would not put up with any nonsense from the youngest ones, and that each of them would be working hard this morning. He figured his mom would be gathering the daily manna, and getting all of the dishes and food preparation tools packed away for however long it would take to get to the Jordan River.

The journey to the Jordan had not taken Simeon and Nathan very long, but they were two young men, in good shape, and on a mission. The logistics of getting over one million people and all of their gear across the mountains was a much larger accomplishment, and would take a significant amount of extra time.

After receiving the order, all the people started moving. Joshua, Caleb, Simeon, and Nathan led the way. Nathan was carrying Joshua's normal pack of items to move, and Simeon was glad that his friend had been given that honor. He could tell that Joshua really liked Nathan.

They had not spoken about the cross exchange the day before, but Simeon already planned to apologize at the first opportunity. He was grateful that Nathan had been with him to share the experiences of spying out Jericho. If only Rebekkah's father knew Nathan well enough to see in him all that Simeon knew was there. He hoped for a chance to tell him what a good choice Nathan would be for a son-in-law, but wasn't sure if that opportunity would present itself.

As they headed out, Simeon's thoughts drifted to his own father, and how difficult this past week must have been for him. His son rebuked the older men, and then disappeared for days. Simeon hoped that Joshua had somehow communicated effectively with both of their families.

What could he have told them without giving away the secret mission? Simeon pondered that for quite a while, but didn't come up with a sufficient story, and questioned whether Joshua could have done better.

Before long, they could see the shore of the Jordan River. *The trip didn't take nearly so long this time*, Simeon thought. He knew that couldn't actually be the case, surely it was just his perception. He must have been far more anxious to see it the first time when his grand adventure had been beckoning him.

The river was even wider than it had been several days ago when they tried to cross at this same spot. Walking a bit faster, Simeon caught up with Joshua to offer advice.

"Neither man nor beast can cross the Jordan River at this spot during flood season," he quoted the men on camels. "Some considerate travelers took us upstream, half a day's journey, to a spot where the ground is higher and the river is not so large. Nathan and I can show you where we crossed, if you'd like. We found the same spot on the way back home yesterday, and it was rough, but we made it."

Joshua looked out at the river and once again seemed to be praying. He turned to Simeon and said, "Thank you, but this is where we camp. Adonai will provide a way, even though there seems to be no way."

The people closest to the four of them turned around and told the ones behind them that this is where they would camp. Those people told the ones behind them, and so the news traveled to everyone. Looking back, Simeon could still see people in the mountains. It would take some time for the news to reach them.

He wondered how in the world all of them, including children and pregnant women, along with their gear, would make it across this swift moving body of water in front of them. He thought about how Moses and the others must have felt as they got to the edge of the Red Sea. It was much wider, deeper, and more violent than this river, and they had the pressure of Pharaoh and his army bearing down on them from behind. Surely, however God planned to get them to the other side would have to be no less miraculous than that day had been.

They set up the tents again, with the doors facing Canaan so they could keep the prize before their eyes. For three days, the people laughed and joked, they ate their manna happily, and the children played in the shallow water at the river's edge.

Trying to keep focused on the task at hand, Zidon couldn't keep his mind off Rahab. He was deeply concerned about her safety; in her house with a window in the wall. He had not seen her since she told him which way the spies had gone.

The King divided his troops into two regiments. One was responsible for guarding the city day and night, and was comprised of the vast majority of the Jericho soldiers. The other, much smaller regiment was to continue making preparations for the New Year festival. The King didn't want to further alarm the people, so he told the men to work as though there was no danger. Unfortunately, Zidon was in the second group of soldiers.

The job that had been such an honor only days ago was now a noose around his neck. The worst part of it was that he would not even be able to stay close to Rahab's house to protect her during battle. He was forced to stay inside the palace nearly all day long.

His thoughts were interrupted by a commotion at the chamber door. He could make out Rekem's voice and could tell he was extremely excited about something, but could not discern what was being said.

The door burst open and the guard announced, "Rekem is here to see you, my lord."

""'end him in," came the tired reply from the King.

Rekem entered the Royal Assembly Room, crouching over as usual, reciting his obligatory niceties, "My lord, oh most holy King, ruler of Jericho, your humble servant begs your forgiveness for this intrusion."

"Just state your business, Rekem." The King yawned widely.

"Oh most holy King, the Hebrews have moved." Rekem waited for the King to ask for more information than that.

The fool obviously enjoys baiting royalty. That's a dangerous habit, thought Zidon.

"And?" The King finally caved in and inquired with irritation in his voice. It was apparent that he did not appreciate being toyed with.

"And they are all camped on the shores of the Jordan. There are even more of them than we thought." This time Rekem did not wait to be prodded. The words almost tumbled over each other as he explained their position, their physical stature, and way of living.

"I think their leader is one of two old men, but I cannot tell for sure from this side of the river. May I have a commission to go upstream, ford the river, and sneak around their camp until I gather more information, oh most gracious King?" He finally requested.

How transparent! thought Zidon. Of course the King would want him to gather more information. Rekem was obtaining a guarantee of payment for his services. *What a weasel!*

+-+-+-+

After three days, Joshua assembled the chiefs of each tribe and sent them through the camp to get everyone ready to cross the river. When they saw the Ark of the Covenant, and the priests bearing it, they were to follow at a great distance.

After three days, Joshua assembled the chiefs of each tribe and sent them through the camp to get everyone ready to cross the river. When they saw the Ark of the Covenant, and the priests bearing it, they were to follow at a great distance.

As the people readied themselves to move, Joshua stood at the edge of the river. With a loud voice he cried out to the congregation, "Sanctify yourselves, for tomorrow Adonai will do wonders among you!" This too, traveled through the masses of people just as his other commands had.

Calling the same twelve men who had assembled in his tent to hear the report of the two "spies," he commissioned them to stay close to him as they crossed; the Lord had need of them.

He summoned the priests, and instructed them to be ready to take up the Ark and cross over before the people. Then he sent them all away with a repeat of his instructions to the congregation. "Sanctify yourselves."

That evening while walking upstream, Simeon was having a difficult time praying because of his scuffle with Nathan. Finally, he turned back to find his friend so he could apologize. He hadn't made it back very far when he could hear someone approaching him. He spoke out confidently, "Who is there?" and was very glad to hear Nathan's voice in response.

Nathan was also heading toward their crossing spot and praying along the way. "Please forgive me for losing my temper while we were climbing the mountain," Simeon said. Nathan laughed and said, "Certainly, if you will forgive me for falling asleep while I was supposed to be keeping watch." They both agreed and began walking upstream together.

"I'm so grateful to have been part of the expedition," Nathan said. "You are a true friend, and I'm glad you are willing to stand up and do what's right. You are always there to push me to be a better person, and I appreciate that."

In response, Simeon admitted, "More than once, I was sorry to have gotten you involved, but was always glad to have you along. I didn't want something bad to happen to you on my account."

They talked about what message Joshua must have sent back to their families, and Simeon confided that he had been stewing over what his father was thinking.

Nathan tried his best to convince Simeon that Obed wasn't waiting around to chew his son out for disrespecting his elders. "I'll be sorely disappointed if I'm wrong. You said what needed to be said, and that's all there is to it."

Simeon was unable to share his friend's optimism. He was still assuming that he would be a grand disappointment to Obed, who expected so much of him. He wondered if his father was just plain wrong when he announced, as a tiny infant, that Simeon would be a man of great faith. So far, he had repeatedly wallowed in the mud of unbelief.

"I'm going to head back to camp and see if Caleb needs help with anything." Nathan said as he waved goodbye.

Sitting down near the water, Simeon prayed again, but this time, he felt much better about it. He felt cleaner. He felt… well… he felt sanctified. And it felt good!

11
THE WATERS PILE UP

Early the next morning, Joshua gathered the priests near the edge of the burgeoning river. Simeon wasn't close enough to hear what was being said, but he could sense the excitement coming from their direction.

Busy packing up Joshua's tent, Simeon couldn't believe today was finally here. It was the day they had waited over 500 years to see. Today was the day all of the slaves had hoped for, and very few had lived to experience. Today, they would cross over the Jordan River into Canaan, and take possession of the land Adonai had promised to Abraham and his descendants.

Simeon speculated they would have to go upstream some distance before they would find a suitable place to cross. Once they were on the other side of the river, it would take time for the warriors to assemble at the front of the congregation and make their way to the gate of the city. He figured they would have possession of Jericho by the next evening.

He hoped they could easily find the scarlet rope, which the pagan woman had promised to leave in her window; then he realized, for the first time, that it was a silly request. They would need to find her home from the inside of the city, not from outside the wall.

Locating Nathan, Simeon asked him, "Do you think we can find our way to the home of the pagan woman once we have defeated the soldiers at the city gate?"

Nathan thought about it for a few seconds, "I couldn't find her house again in that mess of a city if my life depended on it!"

Simeon feared they wouldn't be able to keep their word to her, but couldn't get near Joshua to ask his advice. He was still meeting with the Levites, and now they were bringing the Ark of the Covenant of Adonai near the edge of the Jordan.

Simeon finished packing Joshua's tent and grabbed everything he would need to carry. Remembering that they were told to follow at a great distance, he waited patiently. There were people packing their belongings at the edge of the river as far as he could see in both directions. He pondered how Joshua would move them all out of the way so the priests could get past and they could all head upstream.

Tasks finished, he stood watching the preparations of the priests and Levites with the Ark. It was beautiful to look at. Simeon had only seen it a couple of times, and always from a distance. Usually, it was covered with a blue cloth. The gold glinted in the sun, and he was close enough this time to make out the wings on top. The workmanship was stunning, and he knew he'd never see its equal for sheer beauty.

Joshua's voice rang out, "Come near and hear the words of the Lord your God." The people instantly stopped what they were doing and turned to face him as he continued. "By this, you will know that the Living God is among you, and that He will, without fail, drive out from before you the Canaanites and all the inhabitants of the land."

Joshua motioned with his left hand toward the priests at the edge of the river, "*Behold!* The Ark of the Covenant of the Lord of all the Earth is crossing over before you into the Jordan."

Simeon was caught up in admiring the elegance of the Ark. He almost cried out when he realized the priests were carrying it into the flooded river. In shock, he didn't know what to do as they kept walking further into the fast moving water with it.

He heard Joshua's voice continue, but couldn't tear his eyes away from the Ark, "As soon as the soles of the feet of the priests bearing the Ark rest in the waters of the Jordan, the waters will be cut off and stand as a great heap upstream."

Simeon could scarcely believe his own eyes. The further the priests went toward the middle of the river, the less water was at their feet. As they reached the center, the ground appeared to be completely dry where they stood. Simeon's shock and disbelief turned into awe, and he said a quick thank you to Adonai for his provision.

Armed warriors began to appear from the crowd. He wondered why Joshua hadn't asked him or Nathan to get dressed for battle. He briefly felt hurt, assuming he'd been left out, until he realized these warriors were from the tribes of Reuben, Gad, and half the tribe of Manasseh, whose inheritance lay on this side of the Jordan. Simeon estimated there had to be about 40,000 men of war crossing over armed for battle.

Joshua and Caleb walked across the dry riverbed followed by the armed warriors. After they arrived safely on the other side, then the people all started heading their way. Simeon and Nathan were among the very first to cross over; they moved to the side behind Joshua and Caleb while one million people hurried across.

Simeon wished that the travelers on camels could be present to watch them cross over at the exact spot, where barely a week before, the taunting men had dared them to try. Turning to Nathan with a playful tone, Simeon attempted to mimic the accent of the nomads, "Neither man nor beast can cross the Jordan here. We'd like to watch you try." Nathan laughed out loud.

After every man, woman, child, animal, tent, and belonging of the Israelites, with the exception of the two and a half tribes whose inheritance was on the east side of the river, had crossed over into Canaan, Joshua returned to the bank and summoned the twelve tribal leaders. They each went back into the dry river, found the largest stone they could manage on their shoulders, and hefted them out of the riverbed to the bank near Joshua.

He announced, "Adonai says you are to carry these to where we camp tonight, and leave them there as a sign among you. When your children ask in time to come, saying 'What do these stones mean to you?' you will answer that the waters of the Jordan were cut off from before the Ark of the Covenant of Adonai. Forever, they will be as a memorial for the Children of Israel."

Joshua, himself, then picked up some different stones from the shore and walked back to where the priests were still standing in the middle of the dried up river, and put them at the feet of the priests. He carried 12 stones in all, and then went back to his spot on the shore.

He called out to the priests bearing the Ark to come up out of the river, and they did so. As their feet touched the land outside of where the river had been, Simeon heard a sound like nothing he had ever experienced. It resembled the roaring of an impending flood in one of the wadis in the wilderness, but was significantly louder.

His whole life, he was warned to stay out of the deeply cut canyons during the rainy season. When it rained up in the mountains, above the desert floor, the water would gather in the wadis and come through like a wall, destroying everything in its path. By the time you could hear it coming, it was far too late to climb to safety.

The Hebrews heard that sound every year of their lives in the wilderness. This was a similar noise, but louder and closer than any of them had before dared to experience. The people backed away from the riverbank as quickly as they could. The "piled up" water was returning to where it should be.

Looking upstream, Simeon could see a wall of water reaching to the sky. He could see through it and actually make out fish. He wanted to keep watching it get closer, but knew he needed to move away from where it would land.

Leaning forward as if to fall, the whole force of it crashed down at once, and water sprayed everywhere. It landed where it would have been, had God not stopped it from flowing upstream.

Soaked to the skin, all Simeon could do was fall to his knees and worship the God who was big enough to pile up this large, fast moving river during flood season. When he finally opened his eyes again, he saw that most of the people were on their faces worshipping also.

He was grateful to be on the side of the One who was powerful enough to stop the flow of a massive, flooding river, but also able to control the spinners of a tiny spider. At that moment, he understood the dread of the inhabitants of Jericho. *Adonai is indeed an awesome God!*

Thinking about Joshua and what he must be feeling right now, Simeon couldn't even imagine his condition. The respect he had already held for his new leader was intensified by today's happenings. *What kind of man has enough courage to send the priests and the Ark into the middle of a flooded river, and then lead over one million people into the dry bed?* Simeon contemplated if he would have the nerve to give the command, but hoped he'd never have to find out.

Moses had indeed been a Man of God, and Joshua was certainly filling his shoes well. The respect, almost to the point of fear, was obvious as Joshua headed through the people into the plains of Jericho to make camp for the night. A path parted for him, with reverent silence both ahead of and behind him. Very few people were still alive who remembered the parting of the Red Sea, and even those who did were awed by today's miraculous happenings.

Simeon and Nathan were carrying Joshua's belongings, but were unable to keep up with him due to the throngs of people clamoring to get near him. Finally, they heard the word being passed through the people to make camp.

They continued picking their way through the tents being erected until they got near the edge of where everyone was stopped. Simeon figured if they could get in front of the congregation, they could move around the masses more freely until they found Joshua and Caleb.

The sun was going down in the sky, and they still hadn't figured out where their leader was camped. They were beginning to get nervous about finding him before it got dark.

From way in the distance, Simeon thought he heard his name being called. Standing on his toes, Simeon attempted to look over the heads of the crowd to see where it was coming from. For a moment, he thought it sounded more like his father's voice than Joshua or Caleb, but wasn't sure about that. Hearing it made him homesick.

He was unable to locate the voice, so he kept walking around the edge of the people. He heard his name being called from someone much closer, but didn't recognize the voice. He felt a hand on his arm, and was encouraged as he turned to see his cousin Salmon. "Let me take you to Joshua. He was wondering where you two went."

Relieved to have some direction, Simeon hoped they could get the tent set up before it got too dark. Salmon led them straight to where Joshua and Caleb were talking. Simeon wanted to embrace Joshua and tell him what a wonderful leader he was, but could barely force himself to look into Joshua's face.

This was truly a man who heard from God, and the intimidation was intense for Simeon. Joshua was everything he wanted to be. He was kind and gentle, yet brave beyond reason, full of the Spirit of God, and wise beyond his years. Simeon again vowed to follow Joshua wherever he would lead.

The twelve large stones taken from the middle of the Jordan were piled near Caleb's tent, and Joshua reminded the people of how these standing stones would be a memorial for all generations to God's power. "That all the people of the earth may know the hand of the Lord, that it is mighty, and that you may fear Adonai forever!" he added.

+-+-+-+

Zidon could not believe the account Rekem was giving the King of what he had witnessed. He knew Rekem could not be trusted if there was money involved, but could not come up with any logical reason why he might invent such a tall tale about the Jordan River piling up.

Zidon listened as Rekem described the leader of the Hebrews and was surprised at his advanced age. He was enthralled by the depiction of the brave priests who had walked into the flooding river without flinching. He envisioned all of those people crossing over on what appeared to be dry land. He was puzzled by the account of the twelve men with the large stones from the riverbed. And he despaired at the narration of the great wall of water returning to the banks of the Jordan River.

The King had been openly confident that Ba'al was rewarding them for making the larger statue of him and erecting it in the center of Jericho, by making the river flow faster and higher than normal. He seemed convinced that the gods were keeping the Hebrews on the other side of the Jordan, and had been very vocal about their protection.

The King had heard the stories of how the Hebrew God had repeatedly done miracles involving water, but he had still been certain that Ba'al was greater and held more power over the rains. He had not really believed the stories he had been told, since there were no eyewitnesses who had ever come forward with descriptions. Now Rekem was recounting this experience with passion and certainty. Zidon hated to admit it, but he believed Rekem.

After relating the entire amazing event in as much detail as his vocabulary would support, Rekem grew very serious. "Their God lives in a gold box. I believe I heard the leader call Him 'The Lord of All the Earth.'"

The King stared at the tablet in his hands, steeling himself for the rest of the bad news. Rekem did not delay for the King to draw the information out this time, but continued with a shaky voice.

"Some of them stayed on the other side, but mostly women and children. Their armed men crossed over without them. There are currently one million trespassers on our side of the Jordan. They could attack," Rekem's voice grew quiet as he finished his sentence, "as early as tonight."

Zidon watched the King draw a deep breath. He appeared to be lost in thought for quite some time before saying anything. After lingering over the information, his weak reply was, "I guess Ba'al and the other gods are angry with us for something. Apparently they are not going to protect us. We must protect ourselves."

Finally looking up from his hands, he made eye contact with Rekem. "What did the twelve stones signify?"

Rekem shuffled his feet for a few moments, obviously uncomfortable. "I am sorry, gracious King, but I do not know. I was unable to get close enough to hear what was being said. Maybe they represent twelve kingdoms they intend to conquer."

"More likely, they represent twelve days or twelve hours until they attack us." The King replied, his voice growing stronger. "They will not find us sleeping."

Coming to life, the King appeared energized as he unfolded himself, standing to his full height. He began giving orders as quickly as he could speak. As everyone was leaving the room, he yelled after them.

"They will not find us sleeping!"

+-+-+-+

Lying in Caleb's tent again that night, Simeon contemplated how they would take the city in the morning. He assumed the warriors would rouse everyone in the darkness, and they would attack Jericho while the inhabitants still slept.

He realized there would be no surprising the enemy soldiers. There were over one million Children of Israel camped very near their city. Certainly, they knew the Israelites were there and were ready to fight.

Simeon, who had only seen limited battle with Sihon and Og, drifted off to sleep and dreamed of giant warriors, many times larger than possible, stepping on the Israelite soldiers and squishing them like bugs.

12
KNIVES OF FLINT

Waking the next morning to the sound of chirping birds, Simeon knew it was much later than dawn. He shook Nathan awake. The two of them stepped out of Caleb's tent to a sight neither of them expected.

There were no warriors, no battle dress, no weapons of war, and no trumpets to lead the way into battle. On the contrary, Joshua was sitting in the door of his tent working with a piece of flint. It appeared as though he was making a knife out of it. There were several other large chunks of flint lying near his feet. He was intensely working, and didn't even notice the two young men watching him.

Nathan wondered out loud, "What in the world is he doing? We were supposed to take Jericho today."

Simeon responded, "I have no idea. Maybe he's making himself a couple of smaller weapons in case his sword gets broken."

Noticing them standing outside his tent, Caleb strode over to greet them. He offered them some manna for breakfast, which they both declined. Lowering his voice a bit he said, "I would recommend that you eat something. You're going to need all the strength you can muster today. It will be a difficult day for all of us."

Looking at the kind old man, Simeon wore confusion on his face, "Are you, of all people, questioning Adonai's ability to give us victory over these pagans?"

Caleb's smile had disappeared as he shook his head. "Certainly not! But we do not go to battle with them today. Please just eat something. Trust me."

Finishing breakfast, they waited for further instruction, but got none. All morning, Joshua sat in the door of his tent fashioning flint into knives. When he was satisfied with their sharpness, he rose from his seat. He asked Caleb to gather all the males from eight days to forty years old, and meet him on the hill. They were each to bring with them a fresh linen cloth. The older men were to come along for aid. Motioning toward a specific hill, Joshua headed that way.

Caleb passed the word along to all the men in his hearing, who passed it to the men behind them and so on, until it had circulated throughout all the camp.

Simeon and Nathan waited a few moments until the twelve tribal leaders appeared and headed in that direction, each with a cloth in their hand.

Returning to where Simeon and Nathan stood, Caleb handed them each a cloth, and said, "Go. Be brave. Do what Adonai asks you to do."

They did as instructed, despite their confusion, and followed the other men. As they got closer to Joshua, Caleb's words rang in Simeon's ears. "Be brave. Do what Adonai asks you to do."

Caleb said they weren't going to battle today. *Why would they need bravery? What could God ask them to do that would require courage? What were the sharp knives for?* Simeon suspected what might be taking place, but hoped he was wrong.

God wanted to be in covenant with them, and that would require circumcision. None of the males born in the wilderness had been circumcised. God stated that they would know His rejection. Now, His rejection had ended. They were in His promised land.

Simeon had only heard about what it involved, but wasn't sure if the hearsay was accurate. As his stomach sank, he hoped he had been misinformed, but feared he hadn't.

Hearing the sounds of the men in front of him, only bravery, a sense of duty, and a desire to be in covenant with his God kept Simeon standing in line. Several men in front of him had passed out, and others had gotten sick just from the anticipation of what was to come.

Simeon was suddenly and painfully aware of the sun on his forehead, and wondered why it was so much warmer today than it had been yesterday. *My mouth is so dry. If only I could get a drink. It's so hot out here.* His knees began to grow weak, and everything started spinning. The next thing he knew, he was waking up inside Caleb's tent.

Wondering what kind of dream he just had, he rolled over to go back to sleep. A pain hit him like nothing he had ever experienced, and he cried out in distress. Caleb appeared and put a cold, wet cloth on his forehead. "It will be okay. You just rest now and you'll be all right."

+-+-+-+

Hurrying toward the Jericho gate, Zidon knew the King would not believe the tale they had to relate today.

He and Rekem had departed well before the sun was up that morning; half expecting to come face to face with the Hebrew soldiers on their march to Jericho. They had not encountered anyone, and were shocked to find the Hebrews sound asleep in their tents.

Rekem had pointed out the one he suspected was in charge. He had been sitting in the door of a tent working with something that appeared to be stones.

Rekem and Zidon had watched from a hidden position as one by one the Hebrews came out of their tents. They could not hear what was said, but could sense confusion coming from some of them. Several even appeared angry. Since they had not attacked Jericho this morning, Zidon assumed they were unhappy with their commander.

If only they had known what was coming, they would have been far more upset with him, he thought as he and Rekem returned to the gate. Attacking Jericho would have been the easier task by far.

"Open up in the name of the King!" Rekem called out with his nasal voice. The gate was opened far enough to let the two of them in, then closed immediately after they were through.

The King made eye contact only with Rekem, who was the commissioned scout, which meant that Zidon should not speak at all. Acknowledging this protocol, he silently listened to Rekem's account of what they had witnessed, and repeatedly bit his tongue so as not to offer additions to the story.

Every man in the royal hall winced several times during the recounting of events. The King was visibly disturbed by this sordid tale, and was thinking aloud about what this ritual that the Hebrews performed could mean.

"Is it a rite of strength?" He paused, but was not waiting for anyone to answer. He was just musing. "Is it a sacrifice to their God?" He made a face that said "maybe." "Are they gods themselves?" He said this as if he believed that was the case. "What could make all of those men stand in line and volunteer to do something so gruesome?" He was now shaking his head, his face clothed in utter disbelief. "Grown men!"

After several minutes of silence, as the King was caught up in his own thoughts, he said, "What do we do now?" staring at the floor near his feet.

Nobody in the room dared speak. Zidon didn't want to move a muscle for fear that it would attract the King's attention and force him to answer that last question.

Apparently it was a rhetorical question as eventually the King spoke again. "If they are indeed gods, we are senseless to leave the protection of our own walls. If they are not gods, they are the most foolish people who have ever lived. In that case, we have nothing to fear from them."

The King had been staring at the floor the entire time he had been talking. *He must be thinking out loud*, Zidon thought. He wondered if the King had made up his mind.

None of the King's military commanders dared offer him advice more than once. They continued to stand in silence. The King snapped out of his deep thought, noticing they were still in the room. "What are you all still doing here? Get moving!"

They bowed respectfully and left the room. Once outside the palace, they stood in a group, wondering what they were to do. Not one of them was certain about what the King's orders had been.

"He said they were either gods or fools. Why would we want to attack either?" One man offered.

"Yes, but at the end, he told us to 'get moving,' which would imply action," replied another.

"I say we attack while they are down!" Hollered out a younger soldier, hoping his loud cry would get others to rally behind him.

"But are they down?" Rekem asked quietly.

Zidon listened in silence as the debate continued for nearly an hour. The majority agreed the King had intended for them to leave the Hebrews alone, so nothing was done.

No battle plan was drawn up. No marching orders were given. No common sense was employed.

Zidon was aggravated beyond anything he'd ever experienced. The Hebrews were sitting ducks. Their fighting men were all incapacitated. The Jericho army could wipe them out by nightfall. *The King is a superstitious idiot!* Zidon thought as he walked down the street.

Suddenly he realized where he was. Lost in thought, he had instinctively walked to Rahab's house. Standing outside her door, he began rehearsing what he would say. Before he had decided, her door opened and a woman stepped out into the street. He moved out of her way and said, "Excuse me."

"Hello Zidon," came the soft reply.

He looked at her again, and realization hit him. This woman was Rahab. He hadn't even recognized her. Her luxuriant, long hair was pulled up, she was wearing common clothes not her normal brightly colored silks, and had absolutely no face paint on. He stared at her, trying to come up with what to say. "You are beautiful!" was what he blurted out.

"Sure," she said as her eyes dropped to her sandals. "That's why I always wore the paint…because I'm so beautiful without it." Her tone implied disbelief in what he had said.

"I'm serious." He said with conviction in his voice.

"Please, can we change the subject?" His gushing was embarrassing her. "What are you doing here?"

"Actually, I don't know. I was lost in thought and wandering, I guess. My feet knew where to go, and they led me here. Can we go inside and talk?" He queried.

"I'm sorry, but I've got company, and I'm off to get some honey from Zoar," was her simple reply.

"Company, huh? It's not Rekem is it?" The words were intended to hurt her, but they stung him as well. He regretted them as soon as they left his mouth. He almost reached out his hand as a gesture of contriteness, but she spoke before he convinced himself to do it.

"I guess I deserve that." Her voice was so soft that he barely heard her. "Actually it's family who are here."

They stood in awkward silence for several seconds, until she announced that she really had to be on her way.

Angry with himself for the bitter comment, he mumbled a goodbye of sorts, and watched her walk away.

13
THE SECOND PASSOVER

To the best of his knowledge, Simeon spent two or three days lying in Caleb's tent fading in and out of a troubled, feverish sleep. Every time he opened his eyes, he hoped to see his mother's face, but aside from Nathan lying near him in a similar state, Caleb was the only one he saw.

By what he guessed to be the third day, they were both able to sit up and move around the tent with limited success. On the fourth day, they were walking around and getting back to their old selves. Caleb had been gone most of the fourth day, and near sunset, he came into the tent with a smile on his face.

"Come with me. Joshua has invited the three of us to take part in his Passover Feast." If he weren't still sore, Simeon would have jumped up and down with excitement. Joshua could actually remember the night the death angel passed over, and they were sure to be in for an unforgettable experience, celebrating it with him.

Simeon had heard about the Passover Feast all of his life, but God told them not to observe it until they entered the land. The Children of Israel had arrived in the land of Canaan, and it was time to start the tradition.

Celebrating the feast that evening, they went through all the rituals prescribed by God through Moses. Simeon was struck by the fact that Joshua's life had actually been spared through the lamb's blood on the doorposts. He was the firstborn son of Nun.

Simeon wondered what had gone through Joshua's mind that evening as they waited together as a family, in their home, eating together, and hoping they had done everything properly. He couldn't possibly fathom the fear, the anticipation, or the relief the next morning as they heard the Egyptians crying out in misery, but the Hebrew firstborn were spared.

He pondered the requirements God had enforced. *Why the blood of a lamb, of all things? How could the blood of an innocent animal spare someone's life? Why could they not break any of its bones or leave any of it until the next day?*

There were many things about the Passover feast that Simeon knew held a deeper significance. He could easily recite the surface requirements, but that night he attempted to decipher the meaning behind the traditions. He was unable to come up with anything that really made sense enough to share with anyone else.

He had greatly enjoyed the meal with Joshua, Caleb, Nathan, and the handful of other people who had partaken of it with them, but was anxious to see his family again. He wanted to know how their first Passover in Canaan had gone.

It had been weeks since the rebuke at the campfire and their enigmatic meeting with Caleb. He wanted to share the stories with his mom and siblings. The obligatory apology to his father was coming, but even despite that, he longed to see Obed again, and the feeling surprised him.

In many ways, Obed had been a very good father to Simeon and his numerous siblings. He was harsh, that was for sure, but maybe that wasn't such a detriment after all. He didn't speak his emotions openly like Nathan's father had, but despite the criticisms, Simeon knew that his father loved him very much. He was certain Obed would lay down his life to protect his children, if the situation arose. *That is truly love, whether spoken or not*, he decided.

Anxious to make things right with his father and hoping Obed was desirous to see him again too, Simeon said a prayer for his family, closed his eyes, and promptly fell asleep.

Waking early the next morning, he found Caleb was already out preparing breakfast, but not in a way that Simeon had witnessed before. There was a table set outside Joshua's tent, covered with fruits and vegetables of every size, shape, and color. Simeon stared at it. He was afraid to go any closer. It was Joshua's tent, and he hadn't been invited.

Looking up from his preparations, Caleb was sporting a larger than normal smile. "Good morning young man. Wait until you taste what we have found."

He handed Simeon several large, green, juicy round fruits attached to a vine. Holding them in his hand, Simeon was nearly in a state of disbelief. He had heard about grapes, he had imagined grapes, but he had never actually seen them. Now he was holding them in his own hand, and what's more, was allowed to eat them.

Simeon stood there in shock for so long Caleb started laughing, "Eat one! Pulling the firm round ball of fruit from the vine, Simeon bit it in half. Sweet juice ran down his chin and onto his neck before he could catch it.

The taste was better than he had ever imagined. He popped the second half in his mouth, and savored every drop of nectar it contained. He stood with his eyes closed, consuming grape after grape, and relishing the new taste and texture in his mouth.

Realizing the table was full of all sorts of new foods, he took up another piece of fruit. It was much larger, round, and sort of pinkish in color. This one felt strange in his hand. It was almost as if it had fur on it.

Looking at Caleb for direction, he shrugged his shoulders, "I haven't tried one of those yet." Simeon dove right in, taking a big bite out of the side of the fuzz. Again, sweet nectar ran down his chin and neck.

After several more bites, lost in the taste experience, Simeon bit toward the center and hit something as hard as a rock with his teeth. He chewed around it, and figured out it must be the seed in the center.

He liked the grapes better, but decided to try one more new food this morning. He picked up a long green one that was shaped like a rounded stick. Caleb was gone by now, gathering some manna, so Simeon could not ask him about it. He took a bite off the end and discovered this one was not sweet at all, but almost tart. It had white flesh and lots of small seeds near the center.

Quickly devouring that whole specimen, Simeon sat down to look at the rest of the food on the table. He was examining them when Joshua walked up behind him. "Which ones have you tried so far?" he questioned.

"Grapes, something with fur, and a long green stick." Simeon replied with a large smile.

"Ah, and what did you think of the cucumber?" he questioned.

"Was that the one with the fuzz on the outside?"

"No, that was a peach," Joshua laughed.

"I liked the cucumber, but it didn't have as much flavor as the grapes. The peach was delicious also, but so far, I like the grapes best." Simeon said.

"Pomegranates are my personal favorite, but they are a lot of work to eat. You have to extract and then eat the seeds. They have a very distinct taste." Joshua said. "How about you try one for lunch?"

"That sounds wonderful, maybe you can show me how," Simeon replied.

All that day, people were in good moods. The men were healing up and regaining their energy. The new foods were rejuvenating the women who had long ago run out of creative ways to serve manna. The camp was abuzz with activity.

The next morning, for the first time in Simeon's life, there was no manna on the ground, even though it wasn't Sabbath. God had brought them to the land, provided them with food, and stopped sending them bread from heaven. It was as if a chapter of their history had come to a close.

+-+-+-+

Zidon was growing tired of trying to get some time to talk with Rahab. Every time he had gone to her house since the day he saw her going to get honey, she had family visiting, and would not let him in.

He desperately wanted to get her perspective on the latest information gathered about the Hebrews. He hoped she could shed some light on the subject of the ritual where they mutilated all of the men. She had an uncanny ability to put things into a context he could wrap his mind around, and he really wanted to understand this. He hoped she'd have some time for him soon.

Apparently the Hebrews were recovered and had shared a special meal together. *I wonder if it was a feast to their "Lord of*

All the Earth?" He thought. *It couldn't possibly be a feast. Nobody got drunk. There was no orgy. Everyone ate inside his own tent. It must have been just a large meal,* he decided.

Zidon found it puzzling that the Hebrews had not eaten any of the local fruit or vegetables since crossing over the Jordan, until the morning after their special meal. Before then, they had eaten the "bread from heaven" that was on the ground each morning. Fascinated by the concept, he wished he could have gotten close enough to steal a piece of it from around their camp, but was never brave enough to try.

The people of Jericho had been in a constant state of fear since the Hebrews crossed over into the land of Canaan, and the emotional drain was starting to take its toll on everyone. Zidon had not been sleeping well. Convinced they were going to attempt a surprise attack, every little sound woke him.

With the preparations for the New Year Festival suspended, Zidon had been returned to guard duty. He was sent to the gate, as it was the most likely place the Hebrews would concentrate their efforts. The soldiers at the gate were the front line, the first defense, and they were growing increasingly weary as the hours of boredom continued.

Day after day of heightened anticipation was not good for morale, and the men had begun to bicker with each other. Some had fallen asleep on duty. One man fell to his death as he dozed off while leaning against the edge of the stairs.

Part of Zidon hoped the Hebrews would attack soon, so at least the uncertainty would come to an end. The other, more sensible part hoped they would be content to camp near the river for the next year. Either way, the anticipation was eating him up.

If only Rahab would send her family away so I could talk to her! The more he stewed on it, the angrier he got. *Why would she want all of her family in her house day and night for weeks?*

Suddenly, the only logical reason hit him like a charging bull, *She must be dying!*

His feet barely touched the stones as he ran across town to her house. He knocked on the door with fury until finally her father answered the door.

Struggling to catch his breath, Zidon managed to say, "How is she?"

"She's fine. Would you like to see her?" came the puzzled reply.

"Yes, please!" he said as he held onto his side, gasping for air. He bent over in front of her door gulping air into his stinging lungs.

"Zidon! What's wrong?" He could hear the fear in her voice as he stood back up to talk with her.

"Can we please talk for a few minutes?" he queried, beginning to catch his breath.

"Okay," she said as she came out into the sunlight and closed the door behind her. "What is wrong with you?"

"Wrong with me? Nothing's wrong with me. Why would you think that?" he said before stopping to consider what he looked like after his lively sprint in the hot sun.

Rahab began to giggle at him. "Why would I think that? Let's consider that question, shall we?" Stepping into the street, she looked him up and down with a discriminating expression.

"Your face is red. You are out of breath. You don't have your helmet with you. You show up unannounced and nearly break down my door. Shall I continue?"

Zidon laughed too. "No. I get the idea. Actually, I came to see what is wrong with you."

Imitating his voice from earlier, she replied, "Wrong with me? Nothing's wrong with me. Why would you think that?"

"Let's consider that question, shall we?" Zidon decided that she did his voice better than he did hers, so he continued in his own voice.

"You stop seeing me. You stop seeing all of your customers. No more face paint. Your hair is pulled up. You are wearing plain clothing. And your whole entire family moves in. Shall I continue?"

Rahab was now looking uncomfortable. She didn't say a word. He could feel the mounting tension. Shaking her head, she began to move toward her door, but Zidon stepped in front of her. She looked at him with a dawning terror in her eyes.

Sensing that he had cornered her, he put his arms around her and said, "I'm so sorry. How long do you have?"

After several moments, she looked up at him with complete confusion replacing the terror he thought he'd seen on her face, "How long do I have until what?"

"Aren't you dying?" he asked, equally as perplexed.

She started to giggle, and then it turned into laughter. She sounded like she was terribly relieved about something. Within moments, she was laughing so hard she almost couldn't breathe.

Zidon didn't know what to do. He stood in the bright sunlight, watching her try to stop laughing as her brother came to the door to check on her. He peeked out, smiled at them, and closed the door again.

As she continued to lose control of herself, his pity turned to anger. "I don't see anything funny about this!" he exclaimed. "I'm glad you find humor in the fact that you are dying, because I certainly don't!" his voice grew louder.

She finally caught her breath enough to say, "I'm not dying!" and then the uproarious laughter began again.

He watched her for a few moments, not liking the feeling of being laughed at. "I'll come back some time when you have your wits about you." He turned and walked away.

14
WARRIOR WITH A DRAWN SWORD

The Israelites stayed camped in the plains of Jericho that whole week, eating unleavened bread, until the following Sabbath. It was the holy convocation prescribed by Moses.

Simeon thought about how nice it would be to stay right there for a while longer. Jericho was not causing them any problems, food was abundant, water was plentiful, the people were content, and the men were grateful for the extra rest.

However, eight days after the Passover, as the day of rest came to a close, the men started making plans amongst themselves of how they thought Joshua should lead them. They attempted to figure out sneaky ways into the city, even though it was shut up tight. Nobody appeared to have come or gone from Jericho since they camped on this side of the Jordan. The men plotted how they could build ladders to get over the walls; they even entertained the idea of climbing in through the windows in the wall.

Because Simeon and Nathan had inside information that would be hard to keep from sharing, they were careful not to participate in any of these conversations, and would always walk away to avoid getting involved in the speculation.

After several days had passed, Simeon thought he sensed some frustration coming from Joshua, who seemed to be going outside of the camp to pray much more often than he had been. They had gotten used to him disappearing for hours at a time, but lately it seemed as though they only saw him for a few minutes each day. He hadn't given any instructions, no time frame, no battle plan, and worst of all, no indication that he was in any hurry to take Jericho.

One afternoon, Simeon had wandered away from camp to escape the constant second-guessing, when he heard Joshua praying loudly, asking God to give him direction. Simeon could see him clearly, although from a distance.

Looking to his right, he realized he could also see Jericho quite well from where they were. When he turned his head back toward Joshua, there was a warrior with a drawn sword standing where no one had been a moment ago. Joshua headed toward the armed man. Simeon quickly ascertained Joshua had no sword on him. *Why is he going toward the soldier, unarmed? Why does he not stay away?* Simeon thought.

"Are you for us, or for our enemies?" he heard Joshua say.

Simeon started toward the two of them to offer assistance if needed.

"No." The warrior replied. Simeon stopped in his tracks. The voice coming from the man with the sword was like nothing he had ever heard before. It was strong and masculine, yet almost melodious. Simeon was immediately at peace, and dropped to his knees so as not to be seen.

"I am Commander of the Lord's Army, and I have now come." At this, Joshua fell on his face and worshipped the man. "What does my Lord say to His servant?" Joshua asked with his face to the ground.

"Take the sandals off your feet, for the place where you stand is holy," the soldier replied. Joshua immediately removed his sandals, and continued to worship.

Simeon thought about how Moses had been told the same thing when he saw Adonai in the bush that burned. He wondered if this could be another appearance of God. *He can't be an ordinary angel, they don't allow themselves to be worshipped, and this being welcomes it*, thought Simeon.

"See, I have given you Jericho, its king, and its mighty men of valor," the strong voice continued.

Simeon's eavesdropping was interrupted by a sound behind him, and he turned to see a goat in the brush near his feet. He tried to silently shoo it away so it would not draw attention to where he was kneeling, but was unsuccessful at getting the obstinate creature to leave. *Goats are stupid, stubborn animals*, he thought. After a few branches and the edge of Simeon's sandal had been nibbled on, the goat wandered away to find somewhere else to eat.

Simeon looked back at Joshua who was now standing with his shoes on. The warrior with the intense voice was gone. Joshua walked away in the opposite direction, and Simeon was grateful he had not been discovered. He waited there for a while, thinking about how much power was in that soldier's voice, and wondering what he had missed during his tousle with the goat.

As the Sabbath drew near and the sun dipped lower in the sky, he headed back to camp, and another night in Caleb's tent.

+-+-+-+

Zidon returned to Rahab's house the next day. She was not home, and her family did not invite him to wait for her. Now, more than a week had passed, and he had not found the time to go see her again.

Resuming plans for a New Year Festival, the King had summoned the men to return to his palace. Zidon had been there almost non-stop since the order was given. He had secured plenty of wine, hired extra cooks, and spent much of his time in the royal kitchen deciding what foods would be needed for the great feast. The festival would start in two days, and last for one week.

The Hebrews have not moved since their arrival on this side of the Jordan, but they may smell my food and come running to investigate, Zidon quipped to himself. He confidently walked down the passageway toward the Royal Assembly Room, to give the King his final report.

Approaching the entrance, he noticed Rekem was hurrying from the opposite direction. They met at the door at precisely the same moment.

"Who should I announce?" the guard asked flatly.

"I have news about the Hebrews," Rekem said to Zidon, thereby requesting preference. Zidon acknowledged it to the guard, who turned and announced, "Rekem is here to see you, my lord."

"Enter," came the tired reply from the King. The guard stepped aside and let both men through. Zidon moved to the side to watch the usual routine with Rekem.

"My lord, oh most holy King, ruler of Jericho, your humble servant begs your forgiveness for this intrusion."

"What is it this time?" the King asked wearily.

Zidon could tell the King wasn't getting a bit more sleep than anyone else in Jericho. He had dark circles under his eyes, and he was leaning against the back of the throne.

Studying him, Zidon realized that he usually sat erect, without touching anything but the seat. Today, he almost lounged in the throne. It looked very plebian to Zidon.

"Oh most gracious King," Rekem continued in his nasal voice, "there has been a spirit with the Hebrew leader."

"What kind of spirit?" the King asked, still reclining.

"Maybe it was their Lord of All the Earth." Rekem appeared to be watching the King for a reaction.

"He was rather large," Rekem said, still gauging the King's posture with anticipation. "It was a warrior, and he was wearing battle gear." At this, Rekem got his wish. Sitting straight up, the King assumed his usual carriage.

"How do you know it was a spirit?" the King asked, a cynical look on his face.

"Their leader, the old man, was outside of the camp, very near our wall, and he was talking to himself. Maybe he was praying to something, I don't know what, the gold box that their God lives in was not with him. Suddenly, out of nowhere, a huge soldier in battle dress appeared."

The King sat in rapt attention, waiting for the rest of the story. "He had his sword drawn, and their leader went toward him, rather than fleeing from him. He must be a very brave man. The soldier was huge and powerful looking. I would have run away as fast as my feet could have carried me."

At this comment, the King visibly rolled his eyes. Even though Rekem was certainly not known for his overwhelming bravery, Zidon was surprised he would admit it to everyone in the room, including the King himself.

"I could not hear what was being said, but the leader took off his sandals and bowed down to the spirit soldier, who spoke to him briefly and then disappeared."

"What did the leader do then?" the King asked.

"He got up, put on his sandals, and headed back toward their camp."

"Why did he take off his sandals?" the King appeared to be getting frustrated.

"I do not know, my lord." Rekem admitted.

"What could this mean? Who is this Lord of All the Earth that they serve? Is he truly more powerful than all of our own gods combined? This cannot be the case."

The King slumped back into his throne again as he mumbled, "I sincerely hope that is not the case."

15
OUR GREATEST DAY YET

The day the descendants of Abraham had waited for was finally here. The men were donning their battle dress and sharpening their swords. Young boys picked up long straight sticks, which became make-believe swords, and were fighting each other. The women were busy fussing over the men.

Simeon had to borrow his battle clothing from whatever extras were obtainable. This left his own, at home, available for his brother Eli who was almost old enough to go to war. He suspected Eli was doing his best to convince Obed that today should be his first skirmish.

While Simeon was futilely attempting to get the makeshift armor to fit right, he saw something for which he was totally unprepared. The priests and Levites were making the Ark of the Covenant ready to go to battle. Several of the priests were carrying shofars, and he wondered what they could possibly need the instruments of ram's horns for today. Moses had not only specified that the priests were exempt from fighting, but that the Ark was not to go to war, either.

Though he was confused about these things, Simeon couldn't possibly ask Joshua why he was breaking the commands Moses had laid out. He reminded himself of the vow to not question his leader, especially after having watched him meet with the mysterious warrior. *Joshua has spoken with Adonai himself, or at least the Commander of His Army, so why am I concerned with seemingly minor regulations being compromised?* Simeon felt foolish for doing so.

It was possible the priests had volunteered for duty, but that seemed ridiculous considering their lack of training with weaponry. Every Hebrew dressed for battle that day had spent years training with a sword, and even longer for hand-to-hand combat. The priests, on the other hand, had used their time learning the rules of the tabernacle and the sacrifices. They had certainly not studied how to defeat giants.

Joshua gave the signal for the troops to assemble, then he divided them into the front and rear guard. He positioned the seven priests with their shofars directly behind the group of soldiers in the front, and the Ark directly behind the shofars. The other fighting men were lined up behind the Ark of the Covenant.

The warriors were not given orders to protect the priests or the Ark, but were rather instructed to not make a single sound as they marched. Joshua said there would be a time when he would tell them to shout, but to go silently until then.

+-+-+-+

"The Hebrews are coming! The Hebrews are coming!"

Zidon could hear the cries in the street. He had been at the palace when Rekem burst into the Royal Assembly Room. He would not even wait for the guards to announce him to the King.

"The Hebrews have at least 500,000 armed warriors on their way here right now!" Rekem had nearly shouted it at the King who looked as though he would pass out. It was the first time Zidon could ever remember seeing Rekem there without the obligatory groveling at the beginning of his audience.

The King quickly ordered Zidon and the other soldiers in the room to the city gate. The adrenaline was flowing freely in Jericho. Nobody in the town was asleep. Every able-bodied man assumed a position on the wall. Several women also tried to take up a sword and help.

Standing on the wall over the gate, Zidon wished the townspeople would be quiet so he could hear when the Hebrew army was approaching. The noise of the city dwellers wailing and hollering was slowly dying down, but not fast enough for Zidon. He strained his eyes and ears, but saw nothing, and heard nothing.

"They are approaching from the East!" came the cry from the watchtower.

Well, of course they are coming from the East, thought Zidon, *the Jordan River is to the east of us! Why can't I hear them?* he wondered in frustration. Usually there was a war cry that preceded every battle. It was to stir up the courage of the attacking warriors, and intimidate the defending ones. *Maybe they don't understand its two-fold purpose,* Zidon thought.

+-+-+-+

The Children of Israel positioned themselves outside of Jericho, but weren't anywhere near the gate. The pagan soldiers lined the top of the wall so thickly that Simeon could not see daylight between them. He thought for a moment that he spotted the one with the shifty eyes that they had seen in the city, but was too far away to be sure.

Joshua told the priests to blow the shofars constantly as they marched, and the Hebrew soldiers began what Simeon expected to be the greatest day in their history. He was close to the front of the group, near Joshua and Caleb, and had made sure he was positioned beside Nathan in the line. Since there was fighting to be done today, he wanted to be next to Nathan with his skilled swordsmanship.

Marching forward in the direction Joshua ordered, the shofars seemed to come to life. Simeon had never stood close to one, let alone seven at once, and the sound was ear splitting. He felt sorry for the men behind him, the ones who were directly in front of the shofars.

Simeon wished he had volunteered to go behind the priests, rather than ahead of them, but kept his regrets to himself. He and Nathan had to be near the beginning of the company so they could keep their promise to rescue the woman and her family from the coming destruction.

+-+-+-+

The soldiers on the wall stood silent and motionless as the company of Hebrew warriors approached Jericho. Every man in the city was on the wall, each attempting to get an accurate count of how many men he would fight that day.

The line of Hebrews stretched so far back toward the Jordan River that the citizens of Jericho could not tell where it stopped. Zidon was surprised that they were in such a formation. He had expected them to surround the city and attack from all sides, while concentrating the majority of their force at the gate.

The Hebrews marched up to the wall and stopped. There was bone-chilling silence for several moments that was broken as soon as the front line of men turned and began moving around the edge of the city. As they advanced, somewhere in the middle of the mass of men, they were blowing on trumpets of some sort.

Those don't sound anything like our trumpets, Zidon thought. *They are so loud!*

The Hebrews came into Zidon's view from around the edge of the wall, and he wondered which were the two who had evaded his search party.

The line of soldiers continued moving past Zidon for what seemed like a tremendously long time. Eventually, he saw the men with the loud trumpets. *Those look like ram's horns,* he thought. *No wonder it is ear-splitting. I wish they would quit blowing those and just shout at us. It would be much quieter, and probably less intimidating.*

The men with the ram's horns eventually passed by Zidon, and he was grateful they were no longer so loud. The golden box that houses their God was directly behind the trumpet-blowers. Wondering why their God was not leading the procession, he also observed the fact that none of the men had ladders. "Do they intend to breach the gate and *all* enter the city that way?" he wondered in shock. "That's not a very wise plan."

He observed the discipline of the soldiers. Not one of them made a sound as they marched. Usually, men hyped up for battle are rowdy and loud. These men were completely quiet.

I wonder how the commander convinced all of these men to be silent? he thought. The same moment, he noticed that not one of the Jericho soldiers had made a sound, either.

Maybe the Hebrews are as scared and tired as we are, he thought. *Most of us stand a cubit taller than any of them, and we have our wall. If I were them, I would be terrified of us, too.*

With that realization, he stood a bit taller and puffed out his chest. Knowing that months of preparation had come down to this moment, he confidently waited for the Hebrew command to attack the gate.

+-+-+-+

As the whole company of Israelites rounded the first corner of the city, Simeon spotted something hanging out of a window ahead of them. Rather than paying attention to the task at hand, he was straining to see if it was the scarlet cord. Beginning to walk faster than everyone else, Simeon nearly knocked Caleb down. His first instinct was to apologize, but fortunately caught himself before he spoke. Caleb smiled and continued his journey.

Simeon was chastising himself for the lack of concentration when Nathan elbowed him in the arm. He motioned to the window Simeon had been straining to see. The scarlet rope was bound there exactly as it had been the night they escaped.

Simeon was relieved to see it, but was also doubtful that they would be able to honor their pact with her. He and Nathan agreed that there was no way they could possibly find her house again. Even if they were standing in front of it, they would not recognize it. Simeon wondered if Adonai would make a way for them to get to her. Otherwise, it would be completely impossible.

He began taking mental notes about which direction they needed to go once inside the gate, so they could head back to this spot in the wall. He hoped they could quickly and easily defeat the soldiers at the gate, so not much time would be lost. He harbored a secret fear that one of the other Hebrews would reach her house first, and then there would be no way to stop her destruction. He said a quick prayer that Adonai would allow them to honor their oath.

They rounded another corner of the wall, and now the gate was within view. The soldiers on top of the wall appeared to be nearly panicked with fear.

Approaching the closed gate, Simeon's adrenaline started pumping. He could feel his hands begin to tingle and shake. He readied himself for instructions from Joshua about how to penetrate the gate, but was confused when they continued to march right past it. As another corner of Jericho's outer wall came into view, Simeon was bewildered.

He wanted so badly to trust Joshua, but was also old enough to understand that they needed to find the wall's weakest point; the easiest to overcome location. The gate was quite obviously that spot. Now they had passed it, and the incessant noise from the shofars was almost more than he could take. He wanted desperately to rush Jericho and spearhead the siege, but knew that was unacceptable, so he continued to march along with all the other baffled men.

They had completed a circle all the way around Jericho when Joshua gave the command for the priests to stop blowing the shofars. The silence was deafening. He then led them away from Jericho and headed for their encampment.

Simeon noticed that there were so many Hebrew soldiers that the column stretched nearly all of the way around the city. As Joshua and the others at the front headed back for camp, the tail end of the rearguard was just starting their journey around the wall.

+-+-+-+

Zidon was steeling his resolve to fight with all he had when he realized the line of soldiers marching past him was coming to an end. The sound from the ram's horns ceased as the men to the sides of him stood in shock. He could see the disbelief on their faces.

Apparently, the Hebrews had changed their minds and didn't want to fight after all. They had turned around and headed back to their camp. There was utter silence as the Jericho soldiers attempted to comprehend what had just happened.

Suddenly relief swept through the crowd, and the people cheered so loudly that it hurt Zidon's already aching ears. People were hugging and crying in the streets. Women were disrobing and dancing in front of Ba'al. The fire for incense was raging. Musicians with instruments appeared. The music started, and a full-blown celebration began to take place in the street by the gate.

The people started drinking and partying as if the New Year Festival was in full swing. In fact, soldiers appeared carrying the jars of wine that Zidon had set aside for the feast.

The relief that the people shared with each other brought them together in a way that Zidon had never seen. Each person in Jericho had been faced with imminent death that morning, but had been given a second chance, apparently through some act of the gods.

Watching the drunken revelry in the street below his perch, Zidon became disgusted. "Is this what people do with a second chance at life? Get drunk and have an orgy?" He was thinking out loud, but there was nobody who cared enough to listen.

Many of the soldiers had abandoned their posts along with all the volunteers who had shown up. Only the seasoned soldiers remained aloft on the wall. There were still several men in the lookout tower, but Zidon didn't trust them to keep their minds on what was at hand.

His eyes longingly searched the crowd below for Rahab, but could not find her anywhere. *That's odd*, he thought. *Usually she is right in the center of the dancing and festivities.*

After watching for her long into the day, he decided she was not coming to honor the gods. His focus changed, and he began to try to convince the soldiers on the wall that they had not seen the last of the Hebrews.

"Nonsense!" one soldier replied. "They took one look at our impenetrable wall, covered with giant soldiers, and turned tail. They knew they were out manned and headed home like scared girls."

"If only it were that easy," Zidon repeatedly attempted to persuade them, "this is not over yet!" Not one of them appeared to heed his caution.

He wished with all that was in him that he could climb down the stairs and go influence Rahab to leave her house on the wall before the sun went down.

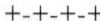

As the Israelites quietly returned to camp, Simeon attempted to decipher why Joshua had chosen not to attack the gate. The only conclusion he could reasonably draw was that Joshua was doing his own reconnaissance with this early morning jaunt around Jericho.

Simeon felt as though he and Nathan were complete failures. They could have lost their lives endeavoring to get information about the city, but they did such a poor job that Joshua had to spy out the place for himself, along with half a million armed soldiers.

His adrenaline had long ago stopped pumping, and now he felt nothing but depression. Nearing the edge of camp, the women came running to find out how they had managed to take the city so quickly. Simeon slipped away to spend some time alone.

Sitting at the edge of the Jordan River, listening to the current splashing on the rocks in front of him, he took off his sandals and dipped his dusty feet into the water's edge. It refreshed him a bit, and soon he felt ready to face Caleb's tent again.

The mood was somber, and most of the men had gone inside their tents to escape the heat of the mid-day sun. Simeon approached Caleb's door, but froze when he heard raised voices inside Joshua's tent. There were quite a few men inside, questioning Joshua about his battle plan.

Joshua just kept telling them he was doing what Adonai had asked him to do, through the Commander of His Army. They wanted to know how and when the gate would be breached. Joshua's answer remained the same; he was following the instructions given to him. After several rounds of this, Joshua became exasperated with their lack of trust. "Enough! If you have a problem with Adonai's plan, tell Him about it, not me!"

After a few moments, the men started to filter out of the tent. Simeon ducked inside Caleb's tent as the first ones left, hoping he hadn't been noticed. He laid down on his mat, and waited for Caleb to return.

16
A SLEEPLESS NIGHT

The following morning, in near darkness, as the men were again getting dressed for battle, Simeon tried to keep his confidence in their leader.

He managed to avoid any discussion with Caleb and Nathan the previous evening, then he slept fitfully. Fearing that the Canaanites would attack them in their beds, every little sound woke him. Simeon hoped his nearly sleepless night would not affect his ability to fight.

The priests, the shofars, and the Ark were positioned in the center of the group of soldiers, and they marched to Jericho. Joshua gave the command for the priests to blow the horns, and the Israelites began marching around the city in silence.

Simeon concentrated on the windows, waiting to see the scarlet rope in one of them, and again attempted to get better directional bearings so they could find her door on the other side.

They passed the city gate, and the soldiers on the wall were still as thick as sheep's wool. After making one complete circle around the city, the shofars stopped.

Simeon and Nathan were closer to the gate today than they had been yesterday at the end of their march. Simeon felt as though he had a better grasp on how long it would take them to get to the gate, and in turn, to the area where the woman lived. His adrenaline had kicked in, and he was ready to get this job done. Glancing at Nathan, he saw the disappointment on his face as Joshua turned and led them back to camp in silence.

+-+-+-+

The drunken revelry inside Jericho had lasted long into the night. The civilians stayed longer than the soldiers, who were exhausted from weeks of heightened alert.

Zidon was one of many who stayed at his post all night. He was convinced the Hebrews would return under cover of darkness. He strained his ears all night to hear their feet shuffling in the dust, but heard nothing.

Judging from their ability to march in total silence as demonstrated that morning; he assumed they could also organize themselves for an ambush without being detected. As the night dragged on, he heard nothing but the partiers below him, and animal noises which his imagination magnified. The sun started to peek over the horizon as Zidon stood to his feet, attempting to shake off the overwhelming drowsiness.

Within moments, the lookouts on the tower began shouting, "The Hebrews are coming back! The Hebrews are coming back!"

The drowsiness had been instantly replaced with adrenaline. Zidon could not see anything from his position except the mountains surrounding the side of the city.

There was a panicked hum of activity in the city as soldiers attempted to put on their battle dress and resume their posts on the wall.

At least we have a few soldiers who actually got sleep last night, even if it was a drunken sleep, Zidon thought. *That is the only bright spot I can think of in this mess.*

His thoughts were interrupted by the spine-chilling sound of the ram's horns. He could hear them approaching long before he could actually see the seemingly unending line of Hebrew soldiers, who marched again in total silence.

He prepared himself for them to lay siege again. Instead, they continued to march past him. He heard the trumpets cease, and the Hebrews headed back for their camp.

There was no cheering after they left today, only an eerie silence. *This is no ordinary army we are dealing with*, Zidon decided. He sat down, dejected and depressed.

The other officer on that part of the wall came over to him. "Zidon, you go home and get some sleep. You were right; we haven't seen the last of them. You will fight better if you get some rest."

Zidon tried to convince him that he was fine, but finally the officer prevailed. Slowly climbing down the stairs, he debated if he should go to Rahab's house and plead with her to leave. As he walked, he decided he didn't have the energy to argue with her, so he went home.

+-+-+-+

Simeon slipped away to the river again. By the time he came back, Nathan was finished eating and had built a fire. Simeon did his best to be pleasant, but he longed for solitude.

Sunrise seemed to come early the next day, and Simeon feared they were going to repeat the past two mornings. He dragged himself outside of the tent and donned the ill-fitting armor. There wasn't a happy Hebrew in the army that morning, and the soldiers on the wall looked tired. They marched to Jericho, blew the shofars, marched around the city, and marched back to camp.

+-+-+-+

Zidon slept through the whole day and night, and was awakened by someone yelling, "The Hebrews are coming again! The Hebrews are coming again!"

Jumping from his bed, he scrambled to put on his armor. He knew he could never make it across the city to get to the gate, so he made a snap decision to climb up onto the wall near his house.

For the first time, he saw the mass of soldiers coming toward the city. He studied them as they turned and started to circle the city again. He felt the full force of the incessant ram's horns as they were pointed straight at him for a while. He got a better view of the gold box, and noticed how beautiful it was. He watched as the column of warriors nearly touched itself before turning and heading back toward the Jordan River.

He was grateful they had not attacked today, but could not come up with any logical reason why they were behaving so erratically.

Suddenly, the thought struck him that maybe Rahab could make sense of it. He climbed back down and headed across town to see if she was home.

Knocking on her door, he wished he had thought to arrange his hair before arriving. It was too late; she was already standing there. He still had not gotten used to how she looked without all of the paint on her face, and was momentarily stunned.

She appeared puzzled to see him, but mustered a smile and said, "Hi Zidon. What can I do for you?"

"Can I come in and talk with you for a while? I could really use some of your famous perspective."

She dropped her eyes, and he could tell she was fighting something within herself. She struggled with it for a few moments, and then said, "I'm sorry Zidon, my family is still here, and I don't suppose you would like my perspective."

"What do you mean by that?" he asked, trying to conceal his hurt feelings.

"I'm sorry. I didn't mean to be harsh. It's just that a lot of things have changed in my life." She was searching for the right words to say, and began talking slowly, with pauses between the words as she thought. "My perspective might not be agreeable to you any more." She began to move back into the house and close the door.

"Are you sure you are not dying?" he asked. He could not think of anything else to say that might keep her at the door talking to him.

She softened, and looked at him with peace in her eyes. "I'm sure I'm not dying."

He watched her as she slowly closed the door. Zidon stood in the street, trying to make sense of what had just happened. Eventually, he slowly walked away, shaking his head in confusion and hurt.

17
A WELL-DESERVED SABBATH

The next morning brought the same routine, and this time some laughter from the self-assured pagan soldiers on the wall. As the days drew on and the silent morning marches around Jericho continued, Simeon became more withdrawn. The jeering and laughter from Jericho grew in intensity.

He was now returning to Caleb's tent after dark, and dreaming of getting hopelessly lost in the maze of city streets. He would always find her house just in time to see a Hebrew soldier kill the kind woman as he yelled to stop, but it was always too late. He wondered if Nathan was having the same type of tormenting nightmares, but didn't ask.

He knew that many of the men were restlessly second-guessing Joshua, but none of them were carrying the burden of a pact with one of the pagan women. Despite the fact that he had witnessed the conversation with the armor-clad being, and therefore had far more reason to support Joshua than any of the others, his "unwavering" loyalty and faith were being tested.

They had now marched silently, with the exception of the incessant shofar blowing, around Jericho for six days in a row. Sundown would mark the beginning of the Sabbath, and Simeon was longing for a day of peace. His spirits were much higher than they had been in days, and he was munching on grapes near the campfire when Nathan sat down next to him with a handful of berries.

"This is going to be the best Sabbath ever." Nathan said, popping a berry into his mouth.

"Yep! I bet the people in Jericho are going to miss us." Simeon laughingly observed.

"Do you suppose the woman has had all of her family living with her now for this whole week? I bet her house feels crowded! Do you think they are getting any sleep?" Nathan replied.

Thinking about it for a few moments Simeon asked, "How are you sleeping?"

"I'm not," came the soft reply. "I keep hearing noises outside the tent. I cannot believe they have not attacked us yet. We're sitting ducks out here."

Simeon hadn't worried about that since the first night. He knew Joshua had posted guards to alert them of any danger, and somehow that brought him peace.

He was just about to ask if Nathan was concerned about finding the pagan woman too late, when Caleb came up behind them and loudly announced, "Tomorrow morning prepare for battle. We leave at sunrise. Pass the word."

Simeon could not believe his ears. They had already broken several of the laws that Moses had given, but now he was asking them to desecrate the Sabbath on top of it all! Surely God did not want them to march around the city again tomorrow.

Somewhere in the back of his mind, Simeon could hear the intense voice of the Messenger, "See, I have given you Jericho, its king, and its mighty men of valor." He immediately sensed peace washing over him. Nathan, however, looked anything but peaceful. The lighthearted joy that he had displayed moments ago was now gone. He stood up without a word and went to bed.

Simeon stayed at the fire for a while listening to the decree pass from one tent to the next. He wondered if the priests were going to join them again, since their duties were sevenfold on the Sabbath. He figured they would finally be exempted, and at least they could have a normal Sabbath.

As he lay down in Caleb's tent, he thought about his own family, and it seemed like a lifetime ago when he was living with them in a carefree manner. He was afraid this whole ordeal had caused him to age more than would be normal. He pictured his own armor being worn by his brother Eli, and hoped to see them all soon.

Early the next morning he rose to find Nathan already dressed and ready. Simeon hadn't noticed before, but Nathan had dark circles under his eyes, and he looked worn out. He said a prayer for his friend, and hoped today's march around the city would go by quickly.

He put on the ill-fitting, borrowed battle clothes, and wished today would be the last time he'd have to wear them, but there was no way to know how many more times they'd make this trek.

The women were not so involved in the preparations any more. Many of them had grown tired of trying to appear concerned for their husband's safety, when all he did was walk there, walk around, and walk back.

All of the men fell into place, including the priests with their shofars and the Ark of the Covenant. There wasn't much chatter this morning; many of the men were protesting their involvement on the Sabbath through silence.

Joshua took his place at the front of the massive column of men and began the march to Jericho. When they arrived at the wall he gave the signal for the priests to blow the shofars, and the whole company began circling the city. As they came back to their starting point, the men were prepared to turn and head for camp, however Joshua kept walking straight ahead and did not signal the priests to stop sounding the horns.

Simeon watched Nathan perk up. He stood a bit straighter and became more alert. All of the men seemed to respond to this new experience. They continued walking in silence as the soldiers on the wall became still. They had expected the usual show, but didn't know how to respond when it went into another round.

Passing the scarlet rope a second time, they made it back to their starting point. Joshua continued walking forward without any hesitation, and the whole army of Hebrews followed. The excitement was mounting; the men stepped a bit faster; the shofars sounded a bit louder!

The Jericho soldiers began to run around and shout orders back and forth. Simeon noticed that there were not half as many soldiers on the wall as there had been the first day. He suspected, however, that there would shortly be as many as they could round up.

Beginning their seventh journey around Jericho, the Israelites were full of such anticipation; it was nothing short of miraculous that they continued in silence. The wall was again thick with soldiers, and there was no jeering or laughter coming from them now.

+-+-+-+

As the Hebrews arrived the fourth morning, some of the bolder Jericho soldiers had decided it was a good idea to mock and ridicule. On the fifth and sixth mornings, most of them didn't even bother to show up. The ones who remained had spent the whole day coming up with clever things to yell at the Hebrews. Each man was hoping his taunt would bring more laughter from his fellow soldiers than the last one.

On this, the seventh morning, there were very few soldiers who climbed out of bed as the guard in the tower announced the arrival of the Hebrews. Zidon was among the few who remained vigilant.

He stood on his feet as the tormenting sound of the ram's horns started. He watched as the men circled the city, wondering how many more times they were going to do this.

When he heard the horns getting closer again, he perked up just a bit. *Did they forget to turn back to the east?* he wondered as the gold box passed him a second time.

"Soldiers! We need more soldiers!" Zidon could hear the commanders shouting. The street below him filled with panic. The fatigue he had felt only minutes ago was replaced with nervous energy.

As the horns and the God box passed him again, he could barely move there were so many men crowding onto the wall.

He could see the energy building in the Hebrew soldiers. They were walking a bit faster, with more of a spring in their step. The anticipation was so thick he could almost taste it in the air.

The box went around again and again, until Zidon lost count of how many times he had seen it.

Suddenly, the Hebrews all stopped marching. The rams' horns stopped blowing. The silence was deafening.

18
SHOUT!

Joshua and the Israelites completed their seventh circle, and came to a halt. Simeon and Nathan ended up right in front of the scarlet rope. Simeon groaned and wondered why God hadn't placed them directly at the gate. They would have to make it around the city to even get to the gate. Then they had to work their way past the fighting, and try to find the woman's house. This would be quite a setback in the amount of time required for them to help her. If only they had a ladder, they could climb into her house and retrieve the people through the window.

Joshua silenced the shofars, stood motionless for several moments, and then commanded the people, "Shout! Adonai has given you the city! Put everyone in the city to the sword. Only the harlot who hid our spies and those in her house are to live."

The priests all let out a continuous, long blast on the shofars and over half a million men shouted at the top of their lungs. Simeon could not believe the deafening sound coming from the children of Israel. The soldiers on the wall were terrified by what was happening in front of them, and every one of them froze as if paralyzed.

+-+-+-+

Zidon stood perfectly still, as did all of the other soldiers on the wall. They were waiting with intense anticipation to see what these unconventional Hebrews were going to do, but were totally unprepared for what happened next.

Not one Hebrew soldier moved. They didn't storm the gate. No one even drew his sword.

Zidon had indentified which of them was their leader. He had seen him on the scouting trips with Rekem. The leader was standing just off to Zidon's left. He heard him loudly proclaim, "Shout! Adonai has given you the city! Put everyone in the city to the sword. Only the harlot who hid our spies and those in her house are to live."

His mind was attempting to process what he just heard. Harlot? The harlot who hid their spies? *Could he mean Rahab? Rahab hid the spies? Spare the harlot and those in her house?*

Suddenly the pieces fell into place. Her strange behavior made sense to him; all her family in her house for weeks, her changed appearance, the peace in her eyes when she said she was not going to die… it all made sense.

Zidon knew that no matter what happened next, no matter who won this battle, no matter if he even died, no matter what, at least he knew that Rahab would be saved.

His mind still racing, he watched in disbelief as over half of a million armed men of war began to shout. They shouted at the top of their lungs. The sound was louder than anything Zidon had ever experienced. He wanted to put his hands over his ears, but for some reason, they would not co-operate with him.

As they shouted, Zidon felt the wall moving under him. He could feel a rumbling under his feet that terrified him.

Suddenly the stones in front of him began to move. Huge cracks appeared in the ones he stood on. All at once, the wall gave way, and he felt himself falling.

+-+-+-+

It felt good to shout, and Simeon continued even when the ground began to shake beneath his feet. He continued to shout as he could see the stones start to crack and move. He continued to shout as the huge rocks in the wall fell out and crashed directly in front of them. He continued to shout as the top of the wall caved in under the weight of the soldiers. He continued to shout as the entire outer wall of Jericho came crashing down at their feet. He continued to shout as the dust and rubble settled!

Silence washed across the Hebrew soldiers as they witnessed the very hand of Adonai crush the defenses of the mightiest city in Canaan. Most of the pagan soldiers had already died when the wall fell down flat, and the fighting men of God all ran straight into the city. The wall fell so flat that none of them had to go around anything to get in. They each ran straight forward, on top of the collapsed wall, and killed everyone in Jericho, just as Joshua had commanded.

Simeon and Nathan stood for a few extra moments staring at the scarlet rope dangling from the window that was still intact, in the only piece of the entire wall that did not collapse.

Simeon was ashamed at his lack of faith. He had questioned whether Adonai could help him find her house, and now here he was standing in front of the only piece of the whole wall that was not destroyed.

She was the reason God sent us to Jericho, Simeon realized. *It wasn't to gather information about the city.* The thought nearly took his breath away. *It was to save her from the coming destruction.*

He could feel the hair on the back of his neck standing up as they made their way around to the front of the house and opened the door to a room full of terror stricken people. The woman, seeing the two men she recognized, collapsed in relief.

Simeon's cousin Salmon came through the door. He immediately went to her side, and helped her to her feet. Simeon quickly explained that these people were to be spared by order of Joshua. Salmon said he was already aware of the oath, and had come to escort them to safety.

"What is your name?" he asked the still traumatized, tear soaked woman, who was unable to reply. "Her name is Rahab, and I'm her father," came a voice from the darkness of the room behind her.

"I'm Salmon, and if you'll all gather your belongings, we'll take you somewhere you can be safe."

She was still unable to walk, so Salmon picked her up very gently, and carried her over the rubble, while her family followed closely behind. Simeon was struck by his tenderness with this pagan woman. He and Nathan helped them carry their possessions out of Jericho and away from the fighting behind them.

Salmon carried Rahab all the way back to the edge of the camp, and gave her family a spot very near his own tent where they could be assured of safety.

When they were given some food and water, Salmon took Nathan aside and talked quietly to him. He motioned toward the center of the camp as he spoke. Nathan smiled broadly, waved at Simeon, and disappeared between two tents in the direction Salmon had indicated.

Salmon then turned to Simeon, motioned for him to come over, and said, "How would you like to see your family today?" Simeon about jumped out of his skin with anticipation, "Oh yes, please!" Salmon pointed in the same direction he had with Nathan and gave Simeon directions how to locate his family's tent. Simeon embraced his cousin;

"Thank you!" was all he could choke out past the emotion blocking his throat.

As he headed off between the tents, he turned around to Salmon, "Take care of Rahab and her family, please," he called back.

"I will. Trust me, I will. She will be well looked after." Salmon replied.

"*They* will be well looked after, you mean," Simeon called back to him.

"Yes, she will." Salmon said with a twinkle.

Simeon laughed, waved, and headed for home. It had been weeks since he'd seen his mom, and he longed to kiss her soft cheek and scoop her up in his arms. His feet barely touched the ground as he looked for the tent with a circle shaped patch next to the door. It was there from the time his youngest brother wanted to see if he could carve a stick sharp enough to cut through fabric.

Simeon felt lost until he spotted that patch. He threw open the door, and yelled, "Mom, I'm home!" His mother squealed, dropping the cup she was drinking from, and ran over to hug her son.

She cried as she held him, looked into his eyes, and cried some more. This routine went on for several minutes until she could stop crying long enough to talk. "Salmon has kept us up to date about you, or I would have died from worry. Are you okay? Do you want something to eat? You look like you've lost weight. Can I get you a drink of goat's milk?" The questions all ran together into one lump, and she didn't even wait for a response. She already had some milk ready before the last word left her mouth.

She handed it to him, sat down, and waited for his story. He drank the milk, savoring the feel of the familiar cup in his hand, and the wonderful smell of his own family's tent. He sat for a few moments, looking lovingly at his mother, and wondering where to start with his "grand adventure," which had indeed turned out to be just that.

Simeon had barely started to relate his past weeks when he heard, "Shabbat Shalom! Adonai did indeed give us the victory! I'll see you tomorrow." Simeon's heart almost stopped beating at the sound of his father's booming voice. He was again flooded with emotion, ranging from dread to anticipation in the same moment. He was disappointed that he hadn't had time to question his mom about Obed's attitude so he could prepare himself.

It was too late. There was a huge shadow in the doorway, blocking the sunlight from entering the tent. Simeon stood, waiting for his father's eyes to adjust to the darkness. It didn't take long. "Son!" He strode over and threw his arms around Simeon. He kissed Simeon's neck, and stood back to look at him.

"I always knew Adonai had great things planned for you. I'm so proud of you! Welcome home." He again embraced Simeon, and held him longer than usual. As he drew back, Simeon could see the approval on his father's face. It was what he had always longed for, and it felt better than he could ever have imagined.

GLOSSARY OF TERMS

Adonai – Literally "my Lord" One of many names or titles used to describe the God of Abraham, Isaac, and Jacob who appeared to Moses in the burning bush. (Genesis 3:1-8)

Ark of The Covenant – Golden "Box" that God told Moses to build. It contained the tablets with the Ten Commandments, manna, and Aaaron's staff that had budded. (Exodus 25:10-22,) It was housed in the **Tabernacle**, and was tended to by the **Levites**. (Numbers 1:47-53)

Astarte – Pagan goddess of fertility. Over the years, and in differing cultures, her name has become Ishtar, Ashera, Ashtoreth, and eventually Aphrodite in Greece.

Ba'al – The name used for one of many pagan gods. Generally associated with Hadad, the god of rain and thunder.

Canaan – The land on the west side of the Jordan River. Also called the "**Promised Land**." It was the portion of property promised to Abraham in Genesis 17:8.

Inhabited by the Amorites, Canaanites, Hittites, Jebusites, Perrizites, Hivites, Amalekites, and the Anakim, who were indeed giants.

Children Of Israel – Also referred to as "**Hebrews**" or "**Israelites**." – The descendants of Jacob, whose name God changed to Israel in Genesis 35:9-12. He had twelve sons who were referred to as the "**Twelve Tribes of Israel**."

Cubit – Standard of measurement that was around 18". It was the distance from one's elbow to the tip of the middle finger.

Exodus – Literally "The Exit." Refers to the Israelites being delivered from cruel slavery under Pharaoh, and leaving the nation of Egypt.

Hebrews – Also referred to as "**Children of Israel**" or "**Israelites**." – The descendants of **Jacob**, whose name God changed to Israel in Genesis 35:9-12. He had twelve sons who were referred to as the "**Twelve Tribes of Israel**."

Israelites – Also referred to as "**Hebrews**" or "**Children of Israel**" – The descendants of Jacob, whose name God changed to Israel in Genesis 35:9-12. He had twelve sons who were referred to as the "**Twelve Tribes of Israel**."

Jacob – One of two sons of Isaac and Rebecca, the younger of twins. He stole his older brother's birthright and blessing in Genesis chapters 25-28. God changed his name to Israel in Genesis 35:9-12, and his descendants are referred to as the "**Children of Israel**," "**Hebrews**," or the "**Twelve Tribes of Israel**."

Judah – One of the twelve sons of **Jacob**. He was not the firstborn son, however God chose to have His royal bloodline come through the line of Judah. He received the blessing from his father, **Jacob**, on his deathbed. (Genesis 49:8-12)

Levites – The descendants of Levi, one of the twelve sons of **Jacob**. They were responsible for the care of the **Tabernacle**, and therefore the **Ark of The Covenant**. (Numbers 1:47-53)

Manna – Literally "What is it?" Bread from heaven. It was on the ground in the camp of the **Israelites** every morning except **Sabbath**. Any excess collected rotted each night except the sixth night when they gathered a double portion for the **Sabbath**. It was white, resembled coriander seed, and tasted like honey cakes. (Exodus 16:11-31)

Promised Land - The land on the west side of the Jordan River. Also called "**Canaan**." It was the portion of property promised to Abraham in Genesis 17:8. Inhabited by the Amorites, Canaanites, Hittites, Jebusites, Perrizites, Hivites, Amalekites, and the Anakim, who were indeed giants.

Sabbath – The seventh day of the week. In Genesis 2:3, Exodus 20:8 and Leviticus 23:3, God set this day aside as a day of rest. Even He rested from creation on the seventh day. No one was allowed to do any work on the Sabbath, including gathering **manna** to eat. Saturday (from "Sabbath Day") on our modern calendars. It begins at sundown on Friday evening, following the model set forth in Genesis 1:5 "...so the evening and the morning were the first day."

Shofar – A trumpet made of a ram's horn. Used for ceremonial purposes in the **Tabernacle**.

Tabernacle – A tent set up in the wilderness as a place to house the **Ark of the Covenant**, and thereby provided a place for the High Priest to meet with the presence of God. (Exodus 25 & 26)

Twelve Spies – Twelve men, one from each Tribe of Israel, commissioned by Moses and sent to gather information about the **Promised Land**. They spent forty days in **Canaan** before returning to the camp of the **Israelites**. Ten of the twelve said that the land was indeed rich, but they could not conquer it, and God killed them for their disbelief. Only Joshua and Caleb believed God's promise to Abraham that they would inherit the land, and were spared. The whole story is summed up in Numbers 13 & 14.

SUPPORTING SCRIPTURES

Genesis 15:13-16 – God's covenant with Abraham

Genesis 49:8-12 – Jacob's parting blessing on Judah

Exodus 17:8-14 – Joshua distinguishes himself in the battle with the Amalekites

Numbers 13:16 – Moses changes Joshua's name

Numbers 13 &14 – Story of the 12 spies and the reports they brought back

Numbers 14:26-38 – Judgment of the men over 20 years old

Numbers 28:18-23 – Joshua's inauguration

Deuteronomy 34 – Death of Moses

Joshua 1 – 6 – Entrance of the Israelites into Canaan, the two spies, Rahab, and the battle of Jericho

Ruth 4:18-22, and Matthew 1:4-6 – Genealogy of line of David including Rahab and Salmon